The Cloud Forest
& Other Stories

John Millard

write side left

Copyright © 2021: John Millard

All rights reserved. No part of this book may be reproduced in any form or by any electronic or mechanical means, including information storage and retrieval systems, without permission in writing from the authors.

ISBN: TPB: 978-1-8382595-9-4
ISBN:eBook: 978-1-8382595-8-7

Compilation & Cover Design by S A Harrison
Published by WriteSideLeft UK
https://www.writesideleft.com

Katipō was originally published in Takahē Magazine

Contents

Katipō	5
A difficult road	17
The tank	28
Stones	36
A short break	46
The cloud forest	73
Something out there	104
Her next door	115
The man in the car	129
One night of love – eve of D-Day	139
Mind how you go	145
The kindness of strangers	163
Vanishing point	185

Katipō

They were preparing to have intercourse, he was pretty sure.

Lying flat under the hot February sky, Peter felt the springy grass of the lawn exhale, grow soft and moist beneath his stomach, as the two brownish-yellow spiders, mottled with black, approached each other on the rough concrete path a few centimetres from his lightly sunburned nose.

The courtship sequence of the common golden brown jumping spider was beginning – just as he'd read in *New Zealand Spiders: An Introduction*. The male raised his front pair of legs, bent them to one side and waved them up and down, performing a neat side-step at the same time, while keeping his eyes fixed on the crouched, impassive female. He began to approach, legs now pointed forwards and tapping the ground in front of her, getting closer now, even closer, and –

'There you are. Your mum said you'd be here. Come on, we're going to the beach.'

Peter heard a swish of skirt and smelled a perfume deeper and muskier than his mother's. He noted a cheery emphasis on 'beach', meant to indicate a special treat for which any 11-year-old boy would be grateful, yet nonetheless a compulsory one. He gathered himself into an awkward squat, reluctant to break free of the gravitational pull of the garden and join the vertical world, and looked up to see smooth calves clad in tights, despite the humidity, and feet in strappy white high-heeled sandals.

'Auntie Barbara, I want to stay here. I'm watching…' He felt strange, saying it out loud to an adult, but it was true, so why not? He was going to be a scientist one day. '… spiders mating.'

Peter could sense the tremor of distaste in the legs, which took a pace back. The spiders had long since fled, but Peter knew without looking that Auntie Barbara was scanning the ground with suspicion. 'Well, you can do that another time, because we're going out. Come on now, your mum's waiting.' Peter sensed a pause for calculation, for recalibration of tone. 'It's a nice day,' she added more kindly. 'You can have an ice-cream.'

And then she was gone, the sandals clacking on the concrete as they receded up the path to the house.

After school every day, and every weekend, the garden was his domain. Long and largely left to its own devices, it had sun-scorched expanses over which iridescent tiger beetles skittered, and shady damp corners that for Peter held the mystery of the native bush in miniature. Inside a rotting log by the compost heap, in a hidden chamber beneath the soft leathery bark, he had found a ghostly white pupa, limbs and antennae folded neatly against its sleeping body, waiting for the secret processes of metamorphosis to run their course. On sunny days he would watch kahu kowhai butterflies – yellow admirals – alight on the hebe flowers and feed, extending their impossibly long and slender tongues for a draught of nectar.

It hadn't taken many trips to the district library to exhaust its supply of natural history books, but Peter had gathered enough knowledge to have learned the names and habits of the animals that fascinated him: the native ones and those introduced to this country, with blind sentiment or in reckless experiments, by Europeans.

Mum and Dad usually left him to it. Often he was up before them on a Saturday, exploring his territory before going into their bedroom and thrusting his latest find under their noses, wriggling in a jam jar. Dad would put down his morning paper and dutifully examine it, maybe even make a decent stab at identification – 'That's an interesting one you've got there: hoverfly is it?' – while Mum would give a cautious smile of encouragement, holding her cup of tea close in both hands and keeping her distance while he explained the significance of the specimen. Then she would move her breakfast tray and pat the sheet next to her: 'Come in here for a bit, love. Put that down over there and have a piece of toast with us.' And he would sit with her, amid the warm smells of toast and adult sleep, until the garden urged him outside once more.

But this Saturday was not right. The door of his parents' room had been firmly closed all morning, and Peter had made some toast himself by the time his mother appeared in the kitchen. 'Morning love,' she said, but waved aside the plate he offered, her eyes falling to the table and the folded, unread newspaper he had brought in. And when she turned to go to the bathroom and ruffled his hair, her hand had lingered, as if seeking assurance of his presence.

Dad was not in the house and his car was not in the drive.

'Your father's had to go away for a bit,' Auntie Barbara – Mum's friend from two doors away – had told him.

'Go where?'

'Work I think. So I thought I'd come and help your mum and make some meals, and do a bit round the house.'

She had been here all day, from soon after breakfast. Glancing in from the garden Peter could see her sitting opposite Mum at the kitchen table, nodding with unusual frequency and force as she listened. Both clutched cups of tea, but his mother's remained untouched. He watched it grow cold in her hands.

Peter knew Dad's job was very important. Testing sheep and cows for diseases was proper scientific work, and sometimes he had to travel far and stay away from home during the week. But not on Saturdays or Sundays. And nor was Auntie Barbara a usual weekend feature.

Adding to the mystery was the deepening of the women's level of intimacy. He knew the rhythms of their conversations in the street: he had listened to enough of them, tugging at his mother's hand to come away, or plucking leaves from a neighbour's hedge in frustration. Now, instead of laughter, their speech was punctuated by lengthy silences, heavy with shared knowledge. If he appeared at the back door to report a discovery in the garden, a sentence would be sliced off in mid-air, and Auntie Barbara's lipsticked mouth would purse for an instant before forming into a smile of greeting. And when his eyes moved to his mother's paler face, her smile too would take that small instant to arrive, and she would say: 'Auntie Barbara and I were just talking,' as if that explained everything, and put everything back to normal.

Auntie Barbara was English like them. But to Peter she was more English, because she had a funny accent – she said 'coostard' instead of 'custard' – and somehow, with her tights and high heels and sundresses and sandals (never shorts or slacks, or jandals, which she called 'flip-flops'), she appeared to resist or even deny the environment she now found herself in, on the other side of the world. At the beach, even his mother would dress in shorts and a loose shirt, accepting of the heat and the more casual culture in which she now lived. But not Auntie Barbara.

She didn't have a husband, though Peter had overheard enough conversations to guess that she'd had one at one time. Nor did she have children. Somehow, he was aware, she had been hurt, and badly. What had happened was a mystery to him, but he sensed that as well as inflicting pain, it had made her defiant.

Another puzzle was why, this odd weekend, she seemed to be in charge. But she was, and this much was clear. They were going to the beach.

It held few enticements for him. The garden was contained yet teeming with interest. The beach was boundless, yet empty. Adults seemed to enjoy its blankness, and found its vacant expanses liberating or relaxing, but to Peter it was a desert.

Once he had searched for shells new to his collection and turned over a few lumps of knotted seaweed to watch the sandhoppers leap frantically about, he was lost. Too fearful of the waves to go into the water, he felt stranded on the brilliant sand, unable to entertain himself, oppressed with shame for not finding it fun.

He was usually rescued by Dad, who would win him over with a kite or a race along the sand, or a skimming-stone contest, while Mum lay sunbathing on a tartan woollen blanket by the floral picnic table and the picnic chairs with their scratchy woven plastic seats. Then Dad would want to wade into the waves and swim for a while, with rapid, splashing strokes, and Peter would make his way across the crusted, scorching sand to the foot of the dunes and perch on a corner of Mum's blanket. She would stir, raise a hand to shade her face, and open one eye. 'Come back to be with your mum have you, Pete?' she would say, or 'Had enough of the beach?' or 'There's some squash left if you want some,' and then smile at him. 'Mind you don't get sand all over me.' And then she'd sink her head back again and settle into the blanket, and Peter would sit with his arms around his knees, watching the sand dry on his legs and feeling the sun bake his pale English back.

And then he would wonder about katipō.

He had never seen one of these small, shy spiders, their black abdomens striped with red, like their cousins the black widows, who constructed their delicate webs at the base of marram grass clumps in the dunes, or in tin cans left behind by picnickers. From his reading he had learned that their name meant 'night stinger', indicating that Māori people feared their supposedly fatal bite as much as Europeans. He wondered if they were as deadly as his school friends believed: whether the playground tales of writhing sunbathers, clutching blackened, ballooning limbs, were based on any truth at all. Should he, a follower of science, who had read nearly all 250 pages of *New Zealand Spiders*, fear katipō? If not, why had he never moved from the corner of the blanket and searched the marram tufts for a web, hung with the dry corpses of beetles and woodlice, or turned over a rusty can, hoping to see the shiny pea-sized animal that was the only venomous creature in God's Own Country?

They went to the beach in Auntie Barbara's blue Austin 1100. Peter thought Dad's caramel Cortina looked the part on the swooping coastal roads, under the big southern sky, but the Austin was dwarfed by the landscape and struggled against the wind. Its sticky vinyl seats, coated with sand from the beach blanket, chafed his bare legs. 'This'll cheer you up,' Auntie Barbara said, presumably to Mum, but Mum said nothing and stared out of the window, and the journey passed in silence.

The women busied themselves with arranging the blanket and picnic furniture between two dunes, before settling down to exchange murmured words. Mum gave him a thin smile and rubbed his shoulder. 'You all right, Pete?' she said, before turning back to Auntie Barbara. Clearly, his duty was to enjoy himself and absolve the adults of any guilt for not engaging with him. He drank some squash, picked at the blanket for a while and then set off, allowing them to talk freely.

As he made his way through the remaining low dunes, he glanced back and saw Auntie Barbara up-end a small bottle into his mother's plastic teacup.

The marram grass whipped his legs as he strode on through the dry soft sand towards the sea.

For a while he patrolled the tideline, wondering at the cause of the faintly yellow scum the highest-reaching waves left on the sand. He stood still and felt the grains sift between his toes and then grip his feet. He picked up a weathered stick and threw it so it spun end over end through the air and then plunged like a spear into the ground.

He wrenched the stick out and used it to draw spirals. Then he walked a bit further and used it to prod a dried and pungent jellyfish. He wondered how long it had drifted in the oceans before being washed up here, well over a thousand miles from Australia, more than eleven thousand miles from England. He threw the stick into the water and carried on walking.

Then he heard Auntie Barbara calling him. Her voice was shrill with desperation, her words fractured as she struggled to catch her breath. He'd wandered further from the women than he'd thought, and she'd struggled to catch up with him. It was funny that he'd made her lose her composure and become breathless. But her urgency scared him.

'Peter, your mum says… Well, look, here's some money. Go and get an ice-cream. What's your favourite flavour?'

'Chocolate,' said Peter. 'No, strawberry.'

'OK, strawberry. Get a strawberry ice-cream. Up there, look, see the shop by the playground, by the slide? Get your ice-cream and sit up there on a swing or somewhere and eat it. Me and your mum have got something to do, and when we've finished we'll come and get you from the playground, all right? Here – go on…'

He squinted at her, silhouetted against the sun, and took warm coins from her hand.

'Off you go,' she said, and there was a note of panic in her voice. She gave a quick look back, towards his mother. 'Go on now.'

He shaded his eyes and followed her gaze, searching for Mum in the dunes, as if she could somehow give him permission to go, reassure him that Auntie Barbara's anxious urging was nothing to be frightened of. But Mum was not at the spot where they had laid down the blanket. She had walked to the top of a dune and was standing in a pose similar to his, eyes shaded, with her back to him, looking towards the car park at the other end of the beach, where they had left the Austin.

'Off you go, Peter!'

With a final look back, he ran to the ice-cream kiosk.

There was a small queue, but even though he had time to sort the coins and present the right change, he fumbled and dropped some into the sand, causing a man in a black vest behind him to tut. Then he had his ice-cream, and busied himself licking off the drips around the top of the cone while he puzzled over Auntie Barbara's instructions. Why did she want him to stay away while she and Mum did whatever they had to do? What was going on? Was Mum all right?

Drips ran down his fingers as he thought. He didn't want to sit by himself, not this weekend, when things weren't right. He wanted to be with Mum. Maybe she'd like it if he broke off the bottom of his cone and made her a mini ice-cream of her own, just like she used to do for him when he was little.

Ignoring Auntie Barbara's instruction to wait in the playground, he set off to their spot in the dunes, walking quickly. The sun was still high in the unforgiving sky, and in the glare he found it hard to locate the hollow where they had settled. Shielding his eyes and licking the fast-melting ice-cream, he eventually spotted the blanket and the picnic chairs. No sign of Mum, or Auntie Barbara.

No, there was Auntie Barbara. She was striding up above the dunes to the car park, but not to her Austin, which Peter could see in the far corner. And there was Mum, talking to someone, waving her arms… And Auntie Barbara was coming up to them, and they were standing by a caramel-coloured Cortina, and the other person was Dad, and he had his car door open, and his hands on his hips, and he was saying something to Mum and shaking his head…

Peter dealt with the worst of the drips on his ice-cream and broke into a trot. The firm damp beach gave way to deep, powdery sand mixed with blackened twigs and litter, studded with tufts of marram grass.

His feet struggled to find purchase as he searched for a path through the dunes to the car park. He could still see the group of adults, Auntie Barbara standing slightly away from Mum and Dad, and he wanted to shout to them, to tell them he was coming, but he was out of breath and he had to keep glancing at his ice-cream to lick the drips, and then he stumbled and suddenly all that was left in his hand was a cone, and all that was left of the ice-cream was a pool sinking into the soft sand, and hot tears were welling in his eyes.

He dropped the cone and set off, panting and sobbing, up the dune, running his hardest now, squinting up into the sun through his tears, just making out the scene: Dad getting back into his car, his hand on the door, Mum moving closer to Auntie Barbara, who was putting her arm around her. The sky's brightness was a dazzling screen in front of him, searing his eyes if he tried to look up for too long.

Nearing the edge of the car park, Peter glimpsed the Cortina's door close in the same instant that he felt a jab of pain in the sole of his right foot and sprawled into the rough grass. Grabbing his ankle, he saw sticky beads of blood beginning to seep from under his big toe, as pain pulsed through his foot and into his leg.

He could see Mum and Auntie Barbara coming now. They loomed over him, out of the burning sky. 'Mum,' he said. He had to explain, but it was so hard to talk through his rasping sobs. 'Mum, I trod on a katipō and it bit me. And I dropped… I dropped my ice-cream.'

§

Mum, Auntie Barbara, the doctor, all agreed that he had stood on a broken bottle, that it was terrible the way people chucked their rubbish on the beach, that he was lucky it hadn't gone through a tendon. He had three days off school, and a lot of ice-cream.

Soon it would be autumn in the garden. Already, when he padded out in his slippers on weekend mornings, the spiralled snares of the fat orb-web spiders were shining with dew. There were new discoveries to be made.

But Dad wasn't coming back.

A difficult road

Tom was in the way. Waiting outside the office, he was a mute, adolescent obstruction to the flow of other members, mostly middle-aged and older, who were moving in small chatty groups out of the Assembly Hall's meeting room and into the small plain-carpeted foyer.

Why had the Overseer asked to see him?

He moved awkwardly to one side to allow Mrs Wildham, one of the deacons, to replace a pile of hymn books on the bookcase. Angular, apologetic, he shifted again to let Doug, the music group leader, get by with his guitar case.

The Assembly members had spent over an hour face-to-face with eternity, sat in the stubborn evening heat of a summer Sunday. Now, released back into mundanity, no matter how devout, how firm of faith, they sought relief in gossip and light refreshments.

Many carried bibles, with tissue-thin leaves bound in soft, well-worn covers, as they moved into a larger room off the foyer where strong coffee and stale biscuits were served after meetings.

The clatter from the coffee room gave way to a steady hum of conversation. Now alone, Tom stood outside the office and pictured the Overseer sitting at his desk.

Why had he asked to see him?

It had to be about yesterday, and the lady who had opened her door. But nothing had happened. Nothing.

Or at least, nothing he could explain.

It was the last week of his school summer holidays, and he was sweating in his best shirt and jacket. But yesterday the heat had been far worse, when he was out delivering tracts with other members of the small congregation.

It was the first time he'd joined one of the Assembly's regular outreaches in the surrounding suburban streets. The road he'd been allocated was long: the main route through the 1950s housing estate where many members lived, along the flank of a steep hill. On one side of the road, you walked down a few steps to the front doors. On the other side, you walked up about a dozen.

Many of the paths on this side had railings to help elderly residents haul themselves up to their doors. The shrubs and trees of the front gardens, even the grass, seemed to struggle against gravity, barely anchored in the thin soil of the exposed slopes.

He'd been given the steep side, and about two thirds of the way along, sweating and tired, had approached a house with a front porch.

The sun was relentless as he climbed the steps. The dazzling clear sky was like a lens, magnifying and intensifying its heat. Below, in the street, cats stretched out under cars, flattened, their territories shrunk to a precious plot of cool asphalt.

The porch door was open and Tom was tempted to simply drop the tract inside. But he stepped in, into the porch's mustiness, where it was even hotter. Avoiding two or three faded fliers, crisping in the sun, he put the brightly coloured leaflet through the letterbox of the front door itself. This was the Lord's work. You had to be sure of delivery.

He stepped back on to the path, breathing hard. Then there was a flickering shape in a rippled glass panel next to the letterbox, and someone picked up the tract and opened the front door in one quick motion.

The Overseer had told them to welcome opportunities to talk to people, to seek conversations about spiritual things. But the woman opening her door seemed in no mood for discussion. She emerged with the tract in her hand, thrusting it towards him, and he prepared himself for one more harsh rebuff. There had been a few already today, from sharp-faced, exhausted mothers and from men in vests who resented the interruption to their football viewing. He steeled himself, preparing to be told to take the tract back: take it, and get lost.

But then her slender arm, freckled beneath a light tan, fell to her side. Tom glanced up and, instead of hostility, met a penetrating stare which searched his face. Her features were open, questioning, her lips slightly apart. She was looking at him, but also beyond him. Into her own thoughts.

After several moments she seemed to recover herself. 'Must be hot work,' she said, and smiled. Late 30s, denim shorts and a pale green top with thin straps. He nodded and glanced away, unable to hold her gaze.

'You've been delivering these all round the estate?' She gestured up and down the street with the tract. Tom looked back at the expanse of road he had covered, relieved that her focus had widened. A tired yellow hatchback slumped on her drive, somehow resisting sliding down to the pavement. Dandelions struggled out through cracks and sprawled, exhausted, on the baking concrete.

'Yes.' He felt himself get even warmer. His shirt stuck to his back and his feet were molten in his school shoes. 'We call them tracts,' he added, dully, unable to think of anything else.

'Tracts, yes.' She paused, distant again, as if remembering. 'You must be worn out. How many houses have you done?'

'Umm… I don't know.' He wondered if this was a failing, not keeping count. 'My bag was full' – he shrugged his heavy backpack from his shoulder and peered inside – 'and now it's about half-empty.'

'And who's "we"? "We call them tracts," you said.'

'The Lord's Assembly, in Grafton Street. The tracts are about what we believe.' He was more confident now, on familiar ground. 'And on the back there's a prayer, see?' She turned the leaflet over. 'You can pray to start your Journey with God, and…'

'How old are you?'

'Nearly seventeen. I started my Journey last year.'

'OK.' Another pause, and another easy smile. But in the soft lines of that open face, Tom could see something else – something he couldn't quite interpret. Maybe it was pain.

Hands on hips, still holding the tract, she scanned the road again. 'And there are other people delivering, are there?'

'Yes,' said Tom, 'but the man I was with, David, he got ahead of me a bit, because he's done this before, and I got to the side of the road with all the steps, so I was a bit slower. I, uh…'

'What?' But then he could think of nothing to say at all, and a flush spread over his face.

Now, the following day, waiting outside the Overseer's office, he pictured her on her doorstep, two steps above him. The strappy sandals, the worn red varnish on her toes, the bare tanned legs and the pale green top. The searching, intense gaze.

The door to the office opened and he was beckoned in. The Overseer was in his late forties. His suits were cut in the current style but were not too much of the moment. His ties were of good quality, but were not ostentatious. His deep brown eyes, luxuriant dark hair and flashing smile went some way to softening his stern features, which were set off by fashionably thick-framed glasses.

He was a popular pastor, regarded as approachable and modern, yet sound in teaching, and Tom was vaguely aware that many of the women in the congregation admired his easy manner and commanding looks.

Addressing the Assembly, his charm and quiet authority would put his listeners at ease. But there were times in his sermons when he would pause and let his smile slowly die. Gripping the plain wooden lectern with one hand and brandishing his bible with the other, his voice rising, rising, as the congregation stiffened in their seats, bracing themselves, flinching, he would give vent to his disgust at the present age and its sicknesses, from which none were immune. None, he would add bitterly, and his eyes would slash across the room, sparing no one.

Then, audibly panting in the stillness that followed, he would place the bible back down, brush a few loose, sticky strands of hair from his forehead, and calmly announce the next hymn.

A nod instructed Tom to take the chair in front of the desk. 'Thanks for coming in,' the Overseer said, putting on his glasses and taking his seat. On the wall behind him was a framed certificate from the governing Central Assembly over in Minnesota, awarding him his title. He said nothing. Tom wondered if this was a pause before an opening prayer. But there was none.

Then: 'Your mum's having a coffee next door?'

'Yes.'

'Good, good. So we've got a few minutes for a chat.' The Overseer raised his expressive eyebrows and the brown eyes glinted. The message was clear: We're going to talk man to man, you and I.

Tom rubbed sweating palms on his best trousers. 'Yes.'

'Good, good,' said the Overseer, running his fingers through his hair. 'Now, yesterday, you were delivering in… Glendale Avenue, was it?' He looked up and Tom nodded. 'And David, he was doing the other side. Now, he says he lost you. You disappeared and when he finished his side of the road, he went back and couldn't find you. He was worried. And your mum was worried, because you were late.'

No, thought Tom, she had hardly mentioned it. 'Well, I got talking to someone in one of the houses,' he said. 'A lady.'

'Yes, so I understand from your mum. She says this lady asked you in, and gave you a drink?' Eyebrows again. Brown eyes on him.

'Yes,' said Tom. 'Juice.'

'And she was called… Julie, I think your mum said.'

'Yes.'

'So, I just need to be clear on a few things.'

'We just talked a bit,' said Tom. Too quickly, somehow.

'Yes,' said the Overseer, 'of course.' He took off his glasses and rubbed the bridge of his nose. Was it number 514?' More direct now.

'I don't know, sorry. But it was a long way down the road, so maybe.'

'Green front door?'

'Yes.'

A pause. 'Fiesta outside? Yellow?'

'Yes.'

The Overseer glanced down and rubbed his nose again. After a while he said: 'So, talk me through it. What happened.'

Tom again recalled her standing there, framed in her doorway. 'Come in,' she had said, 'just for a bit. Let me give you a cold drink – you must be boiling out there.'

He remembered the pungent scent of potted geraniums as he entered the porch. He remembered her perfume in the hot, still air as he followed her down the hall. In the kitchen she had put the tract down on the worktop and taken out two tumblers.

'What do you think of it?' he asked her. She filled

the tumblers with orange juice then picked up the leaflet again. The title, *Good News for TODAY*, burst garishly from a heaven streaming with light. Deep within the source of this radiance, just sketched in, emerged the glittering towers of a celestial city.

'The new Jerusalem,' she said quietly, half to herself, then looked up. 'You know Revelation? The new Jerusalem comes down to earth at the end?'

'Yes,' Tom said. He feared Revelation. He felt lost in its stark and terrible universe. He wanted to tell her that he felt a crushing burden, knowing the truth while others blundered towards the awful abyss it depicted.

'There will be no more death or mourning or crying or pain,' she said.

'Sorry?'

'That's what Revelation says. There won't be any more death or crying. Not any more.'

'No. Sorry, yes, that's right.' No more words would come.

She picked the tumblers up and moved to the back door. Tom followed her out on to a patio, where white plastic chairs surrounded a glass-topped table. 'Just a minute,' she said, and wiped the table with a cloth. The neck of her top hung open. 'There, right. Sit down. I'm Julie, by the way.'

'Oh, Tom. Pleased to meet you.'

'Pleased to meet you, Tom. Cheers.' They both took a sip. 'Your mum and dad, do they go to the Assembly too?'

'My mum. My dad died last year. That's when Mum started going.'

'I'm sorry,' she said. 'I bet she finds things hard.'

'Yes. But the Assembly, the people there, they've been really nice. Once, it was before Christmas, Mum didn't have much money, and I knew she was worried. And she never said anything, but one day after the meeting the treasurer gave her an envelope. £50 from the collection.'

The lady, Julie, had nodded, as if she knew what he meant. Tom had taken a long, cool gulp.

When he had finished his juice, she had offered him more. He had said no, thank you, he had to finish his leaflets. She walked with him down the hall. 'Um… thanks again for the drink,' he said, heaving his backpack on again. 'Better get on…'

'Nice to meet you,' she said, fixing him with that gaze once more. 'Take care.' And she had gently closed the door.

He told the Overseer about the drink and the conversation. He left in the bit about the envelope. But he decided not to mention Revelation, or the pale green top.

The Overseer tapped his glasses several times on the desk and took a deep breath.

'This lady,' he said. 'Julie.'

'Yes.' Pause.

'She, uh, used to be a member here, at the Assembly. Before you and your mum started coming. Some years ago.' Under the desk, the Overseer's foot tapped rapidly. 'She was separated, and she had, what you might call… a relationship. With a… member of the congregation – a senior member. It caused some, uh, difficulty. In the end, it was best she left. Best there was no more… contact.'

There was a silence. Tom shifted in his chair as a chilled drop of sweat crept down his back.

The Overseer's foot stopped tapping. He studied the lenses of his glasses, then put them back on and stared at Tom with renewed force. 'How did she seem?' he asked. 'How was she?'

'She was nice,' Tom said. 'Friendly.' The Overseer's gaze made it clear. He needed more.

'I think, maybe, she was a bit sad,' Tom said. Still the unyielding stare. There's more, it said. Tell me.

'And it was a bit weird' he added. 'She kept looking at me. Staring.'

The older man suddenly pushed himself forward, palms on the desk and eyes narrowed.

'Thought you were in there, did you? Fancied your chances?' His voice bore the fearful intensity of the pulpit, but also the snarling edge of a late-night challenge in a pub car park.

Tom felt hot breath on his face. He struggled to stop tears.

'I wouldn't flatter yourself, mate,' the Overseer said. 'She doesn't go for teenagers. Prefers the older man.'

A dreadful silence. The Overseer breathed heavily, eyes fixed on his desk. An unbearable time elapsed before he eventually looked up. His breathing now was calmer, and his voice was once more controlled and measured. 'You know why she was looking at you, don't you?'

'No, I…'

'Her son. He was about your age. Actually, you're the spit of him. He was on the back of a motorbike with an older lad, and they came off the road, hit a tree. He died. Seeing you, it must have been a shock. And then she realised you'd come from here. All a bit much, probably.'

Tom stared at his feet and wiped his nose with the back of his hand.

The Overseer sat back in his chair and raked his hand through his hair. He gave a ragged sigh. After several moments he coughed and stood up. 'Right,' he said. 'You'd better get back to your mum.'

Tom turned and opened the door, preparing for the chatter of the coffee room.

He would think of something to tell his mother to explain his time in the office.

And he would pray to be given a less difficult road.

The tank

Coolness against the knuckle of his left forefinger as he strokes the glass of her tank.

Quietness at the back of the biology lab as he watches her glide through the still water and nose the side of the aquarium. She is *Xenopus laevis*, African clawed frog. Beady eyes, grinning insatiable mouth. She watches him watching her, through water and glass, across the gulf between elements, across aeons of evolutionary time.

'Here,' he says, 'here you are.' And dangles a worm over the water, watching her kick to the surface. He drops it in and watches her swiftness, her satisfaction. Seizing and gulping, stuffing the prey in with her hands.

He is unformed, ungainly, unplaced. Spending morning break time here, with the biology department's new acquisition, not with his early-adolescent peers in the playground.

She is ugly-beautiful, swooping around her tank in

graceful loops, then floating to her customary resting position, poised just below the surface, only turreted eyes and tiny nostrils above water level. Perfectly evolved. A triumph of the planet's processes.

Cool glass on his finger. A shift in the air as the door opens. He turns, unsure, unprepared.

'All right Harry?' asks Mr Mullen, deputy head of biology. 'Not going out?'

Harry straightens, brushes a lank fringe across his forehead. His hands are lost, looking for a home. One goes in his pocket, another flutters around his bottom lip.

'I'm OK here, sir. You said I could feed the Xenopus.'

'Yes, but that doesn't take long. You've fed her, yeah?' A nod. The fringe slips down. 'Then you should be outside. With your mates.'

Mates, thinks Harry. A fiction they both maintain. There's a shared glance, but neither smiles.

'I like being here, sir. Watching her.'

'OK. But you need to go outside now.'

Harry drops his head, ignoring his fringe. He thinks, looks up. 'Sir?'

'What is it? Come on, I'm supposed to be out there, on duty.'

'Sir, you know that essay I did last term, the one about Darwin?'

'Yes, good piece of work. Gave you an A, didn't I?'

'B plus,' says Harry. Now a smile from the teacher. 'Anyway,' the boy says, 'I'm reading some of those books on him you said I should try. You know the "warm little pond" thing he writes about?'

Mr Mullen sighs, looks at the clock on the wall, rubs

his chin. He is more patient with Harry than his colleagues. He knows this is a delaying tactic. 'Rings a bell,' he says. 'You mean, like the primordial soup idea, all the building blocks of life kind of swirling about?'

'Yes. The warm little pond where life started. But it's what he said after that – I can't stop thinking about it.'

'Harry, this is an interesting conversation, but not now, OK?' Mr Mullen is reaching for the handle of the door into the corridor. 'Come on now.'

'No, I mean, sir, I just wanted to say... It's amazing, what Darwin said. You know, that even now, the same thing's happening, all the time. Life being created in little ponds, only we're not aware of it.'

Mr Mullen considers this, nods. 'You're right Harry, it's amazing. Now come on. Out.'

Harry shuffles across the scuffed floor. The school badge on his blazer, almost ripped off by an older boy two weeks ago, has not yet been sewn back on. Mr Mullen pauses. 'Look, tell you what,' he says. 'How would you like to look after her in the holidays? The Xenopus. Take her home for the summer.'

'Take her home? Seriously?' Harry glances back at the tank, eyes alight.

'It'd be a bit tricky moving the tank, but what do you think? Has your mum got a car?'

Harry is silent, unwilling to admit to an obstacle. 'Well, I could probably bring it round,' says Mr Mullen. 'Is there somewhere you could put it?'

'Yes sir, my bedroom,' Harry says. 'I could look after her. I'd really like that.'

'Well, you'll have to ask your mum, won't you?'

'Yes sir.'

'OK. Now, playground for the last 10 minutes, please.'

Outside. Harry grimaces as chaos and clamour assault his senses. He is not adapted to this environment, he thinks. A football slams into the wall by his ear and its owner appears, shoves him aside. And tells him: 'You're right by the goal, dickhead.' Ten minutes pass like a geologic era.

§

Fish fingers for tea. His mother has had a long day on the till at the DIY store. Sitting opposite him at the kitchen table, she puts down her knife and fork and rubs her knuckles into her eyes, considering his request.

'The what?' she says.

'Xenopus. It's a frog. It lives in the water in an aquarium, and you feed it worms. I like looking at it. It'd be in my bedroom and it wouldn't make a mess.'

'Worms?'

'It's a frog, that's what it eats.'

'In your bedroom.' She places her index fingers on her temples, traces gentle circles on her hairline.

She breathes in, out, heavily, and gets up to clear the two plates. 'Sorry, Harry, no. I don't want it in the house, all smelly and slimy, all summer. We can go to the aquarium in town again and you can look at all those things. But not in here.'

'But it won't be smelly. And I'll look after it.'

'You mean, like when you had the gerbil, and I ended up doing everything?' She is shocked by the harshness, the weariness, she hears in her voice. She reaches out to ruffle his hair.

'Chinchilla, not gerbil,' he says, and jerks away. 'And I'm older now.'

She walks across the room, puts the plates in the sink and rests with hands on the edge of the counter for a moment, her back to her son. 'Harry... It's just one more thing to think about, and I can't deal with it right now. I just haven't got the time. When you're older, and running a house and working, you'll understand. Maybe if your dad was still here…'

But he has gone up to his room.

§

We're in an experiment, he thinks, and this is an observation tank. The school, built in the late 1960s, has gigantic window panels linked by spindly steel columns, giving views of concrete, asphalt and more glass.

The building is mercilessly cold in the winter. Now, the heat of the summer sun collects and concentrates in the corridors and classrooms and the air is thick, tangy with adolescent sweat. Students puff out their cheeks, pull at their sticky shirts. They put down their pens, wipe their hands on their uniforms and pick them up again.

Break time once more. Harry hurries to the lab, hoping to catch Mr Mullen before he leaves for playground duty. The teacher, sleeves rolled up and tie loosened, is placing worksheets on desks ready for the next lesson.

'I'm not allowed to have the Xenopus,' Harry says from the doorway. 'Sorry.'

'Oh,' says Mr Mullen from the other side of the room. 'That's a shame.' A pause. 'Well, look, maybe I could have her.' He reaches the last desk and walks back. 'Or I could just ask the caretaker to keep an eye on her over the holidays. Change her water every few days, give her some worms.'

Harry is unresponsive. 'Come in,' Mr Mullen says. He crouches to the boy's height and waits for eye contact. 'Look, I'll get something sorted. I haven't got time at the moment, but end of term isn't until next week. Don't you worry. OK?' He straightens up, smiles. 'Look, why don't you feed her now?'

Harry does. This time Mr Mullen lets him stay in the lab all break time.

§

Cool water bearing up his body, dissolving gravity. Hot sun on his pale, acned shoulders.

Harry floats face down in the pool, within view of his mother's sun-lounger, and estimates the seconds since he took his last huge gulp of air, swelling his lungs until they burned. In the last few days he has increased the time he can hold his breath by a count of twenty.

This trip to a holiday camp on the east coast was a last-minute thing. 'We can't really afford it,' his mother told him. He knows it is compensation.

Now he floats, occasionally sculling gently with his hands, and imagines the clock above the pool kiosk slowly measuring out his achievement. He is no longer clumsy and out of place in a world he does not understand. He floats freely in a liquid universe bounded by the pale blue concrete walls of the pool, governed by the smooth sweep of the big clock's second hand. Apart from the muffled, distorted cries of a toddler, reaching him from another dimension, the only sound is the thudding of his own blood. Until his lungs burn once more, now with a longing for breath, and he lifts his head, gasping, struggling to focus on the clock through the shimmering air.

He has added a few more seconds to his breath-holding record. But now his mother calls him, and he emerges reluctantly from the water, up the gradual slope that forms one end of the pool, slowly becoming upright as he enters the world.

§

First day of the new term. Salt taste in his mouth as tears and snot run down his face. A world shrunk to a brick enclosure outside the school caretaker's storeroom, where the bins are kept. The wind has busied itself over the long vacation by assembling a small galaxy of leaves, litter and illicit cigarette ends in a corner. Harry sits on the concrete with his back against the wall, hugging his knees, ignoring the summons of the bell at the end of break time.

When the call goes out to find the boy, Mr Mullen knows where to look. On the way outside, he passes the dry tank in the biology lab where this morning, Harry found the starved and desiccated body of the Xenopus.

A tiny tragedy in the vastness of history. One random result thrown up by the swirling forces shaping and re-shaping the universe. A distracted adult mind during the busy end-of-term period. A failure to speak to the caretaker, a confusion of responsibilities.

Too much to think about. The relentless pressure of time.

A small boy and a small promise, broken.

The wind whirls around the school grounds, seeking new playthings, as Mr Mullen walks to Harry's habitual hiding place, wondering what to say.

Stones

So we're down at the little beach, where you can skim the smooth flat stones, all warm from the sun, or go for a swim if it's really hot, or just hang out – and this lady just comes up to us.

It's the summer holidays and when we're playing down at the beach, spending all day there, it's like we're in our own world, a world with no adults. It's like she's breaking the spell.

'Can one of you give me some help?' she says. She's got a quavery voice, like my nan had – only a bit posh, and a bit panicky. She's coming up the steps from the car park and heading for the bench where we're sitting, on the path above the beach.

She's pretty weird-looking. She has a long purple floaty skirt with tasselly things hanging off it, and an orange top with flowers on it, and a bright yellow anorak. And over her arm she's got a shower curtain, the swishy plastic kind that's horrible when you've finished in the shower and you're getting cold, and it sticks to you and you have to peel it off.

In the other hand she's got one of those old blankets that look warm but they're not, they're not proper wool, and they've gone all bobbly and thin. It's light blue and looks a bit dirty and smelly, like the one our cat, Misty, has in her basket. And she's holding rubber gloves, pink ones, like we've got at home for cleaning the toilet, which Mum hangs over the pipe under the sink.

The lady's hair is a bit mad, blowing all over the place, and she's got a crystal on a chain round her neck, like the ones you see in gift shops on holiday, where you can choose one for the mood you're in, or to match your star sign, or to cheer you up or heal you or make you relaxed. I don't know what kind hers is, but it's a big one, swinging as she walks towards us, and banging on her bony chest. It doesn't seem to be making her calm, or happy.

I stand up. Harry and Becki stay sitting on the bench but Harry quickly puts his penknife in his pocket and Becki sits up straight and pulls her skirt flat, the way ladies do sometimes when a guest comes in. By Becki's feet is the pile of thin, flat stones we've collected, ready for skimming.

'I need one of you to help me,' the lady says as she gets closer, and maybe because I'm the one standing, she looks at me. I always end up being the leader, even when I don't want to be.

We don't say anything, but we don't ignore the lady or run off. We're polite, but also we're curious. We want to know what she wants. We know the beach and we know where the good hiding places are, and we can run fast, even Becki, so we're not scared, and anyway – she's just a weird old lady.

She doesn't say anything about the pile of stones. A grown-up usually would. They'd get themselves all ready to be angry and say 'What are you doing with those?' like we were going to throw them at cars or people or something.

If she did ask about them, I could tell her about skimming, about the magic, when you let go of a stone and it suddenly loses its weight and becomes light enough to bounce and slip on the surface of the water. And about how it's best to get a pile of stones ready, so you can throw with one hand and keep new ones in the other, to feed to your throwing hand, and have the pile near your feet so you can reach down and grab new ones, so you can keep your rhythm going, keep the stones skimming, and keep your eye in, like my dad taught me.

He was the best skimmer ever.

Anyway. The lady doesn't ask about the stones, she just stands there looking at us and says: 'There's a dead dog.' And she points down along the shore, the way you only go if you want to go to the boat club, over the little bridges that stop you having to jump across the muddy, marshy bits. Not the other way, the pretty way, along the wide, dry path, where people usually go, when they want to 'stretch their legs', or 'get some fresh air' and maybe have a picnic or look at the birds on the sea with their binoculars.

As soon as she says 'dead dog' I can sense Becki hunching up, pulling herself in, wincing, like when you're on the sofa watching a film on telly and there's a scary bit.

'A dead dog?' I say back.

It's almost like, hearing someone else say it, that the lady feels it even worse, because her voice goes even more wobbly and panicky. 'It's down there on the beach and it's been hurt…'

She stops for a bit and breathes in and out a few times. 'Someone's hurt it and now it's dead, and I've got to take it home. I've got to wrap it up and take it home and put something on Facebook, so its owner will see it and come and get it, and they'll know what happened to it. But I need some help.'

I look at Harry and Becki. Harry sort of wriggles on the bench and looks down towards the boat club and I can tell he would like to see the dead dog, and have a bit of an adventure, but Becki looks like she's upset, so I say: 'Harry, I'm going to see. You stay with Becki.' He doesn't look pleased, even though she's his little sister, and it's his job to stay with her, so I say: 'You can skim the stones if you want.'

And I follow the lady, with her blanket and shower curtain and rubber gloves, along the path. She's very bustly and busy as she walks along, but she doesn't go fast even though her legs and arms are going all over the place and her skirt is swishing and her crystal gemstone thing is swinging. On the way, because I really wanted to do some skimming, and also because I want to show I'm calm and not bothered, I pick up some stones and throw them. But they don't skim, they just hit the water and sink.

Soon we come to a place where the beach is mainly mud, but above that there are lots of stones – mainly fat round ones, not many skimming ones – and piles of dried-up seaweed: the kind that has lots of flies hiding in it that zoom up into your face in a big cloud if you kick it. And there are some plastic bottles – all faded and bashed in, but still bottles that you can tell had water in them, or milk – and some pieces of plastic rope. And a bit below the stones, at the top of the mud part of the beach, there it is.

It's lying on its side. A seagull flies off when we walk down off the path. There are some different flies here, fatter ones, the noisy fast kind that make my stepdad Mark angry when they get in the house on a hot day. The dog has no fur. The side I can see has no ear. No proper eye, only a hole with some jelly stuff in it. The body is kind of blown up, like it was a fat dog, but its skin isn't flabby, it's tight. And it's not one colour, it's kind of pink but kind of bluish as well, and it's horrible.

The lady's seen it before, but she seems just as shocked as me. Her skirt has pockets and she feels about in them for a bit and finds a tissue, all scrunched up and a bit nasty, and blows her nose. I don't look but I think she's crying, and I don't like that. If adults cry then you know things are really, really serious, and you get scared and you want to cry too, but they say stupid things like: 'Don't worry, I'll be all right in a minute', and 'It's just me being silly', which are just lies. What they need is another adult to be there, to comfort them and help them – and you. But if there's no one around but you, even though you're just a kid, and you're frightened, they want you to do the comforting and the helping.

Then the lady says quietly: 'Poor thing. Poor dog.' She puts her blanket and her shower curtain down on the beach and stands there holding her pink rubber gloves like she doesn't know what to do next. She wipes her nose and sniffs.

Then she points the rubber gloves at the back of the dog, where some of the skin has been ripped away, and says: 'Do you think that's where someone hurt it? Do you think they hurt it… and then threw it in the sea?'

I start to feel a bit upset too. I don't even like dogs, the way they jump up at you and wipe that slimy snot stuff on you when you don't even want to pat them or play with them. But I don't like what she's saying, about someone being cruel and throwing it in the water and leaving it to get washed up.

I make myself look at the dog again. I come to the beach a lot, with Mark and Mum and with Harry and Becki. I've seen dead things washed up before – a big fish once, and a bird – and I know there are lots of things in the sea and on the beach that like to eat them. The dog doesn't look like it has wounds. It looks like it's been in the sea a long time, so long that it's lost all its fur, and the fish and the crabs and the gulls have been tearing bits off it for a while.

I try to tell the lady this in a way that doesn't sound too bad. I say they've been nibbling it, not tearing bits off, and she listens to me, like I'm a scientist or something. It calms her down.

She wipes her nose again and puts her tissue away in one of her skirt pockets. Then she coughs and says: 'Do you think so?' and tries to smile. I try to smile back, even though I'm upset too. She's shown me this horrible dead dog, and she's cried, and made me feel like it's my job to help, when I could be skimming stones.

'I've got to take him home,' she says, though I don't know how she knows it's a he.

She says she wants me to help her pick the dog up and wrap it up and take it to her car. But I know this is a really bad idea because now I can smell the dog and I can see that it's rotten and disgusting and not something you should pick up and put in a car and take home, not even wrapped up in a shower curtain.

'You can't take him home,' I say, and I make a wincey kind of face like Becki did before. 'He's been in the sea a long time.' I think this is a better thing to say than 'he stinks', and I hope she'll understand what I mean. Just like when Mum tells Mark that her friend at work has been to see a film and thinks it's really good, when what she really means is that she doesn't want him to go out running, or to the football, or round to his friend Jim's to help him do up his boat and drink cans of beer – she wants him to text Karen our babysitter and book up tickets for the pictures.

And it works. Just like when I told the lady the dog hadn't been hurt, only nibbled, she goes along with what I'm saying, just like I'm the grown-up.

'So what shall we do?' she asks me, and then I realise I have to think of something.

My idea is to bury it. There, on the beach.

I tell her, and I can see her thinking about it and realising it's a good plan because it would mean looking after the dog, doing something nice for it even though it's dead, and giving it a proper end to its life.

'Yes,' she says at last, still a bit shaky. 'And we could put something on it, on the grave, so we know where it is, and I could still put something on Facebook and tell the owner where it was.'

So she puts down her gloves and starts looking for a place to dig. 'Here,' she says, and points to a place above the tide line, in the stones.

'OK,' I say. 'We can make a hole for him.' I move some of the bigger stones, then look up, and she's sitting on the side of the path watching me, like all her energy's gone, and I realise it's up to me to dig. Only when I had the idea of burying the dog, I didn't think about how I was going to make the hole. Once I've cleared the big stones away and got to the small ones and the sandy stuff underneath, I'm a bit stuck.

I look around and I find a piece of branch that's been washed up, nice and smooth and strong, and I use it to loosen the damp sand and pebbles where I want to dig. Then I think about getting a big flat stone, one you could skim if you were a giant, and using it like a spade. It takes me ages to find one, but I do, and with the branch and the stone I manage to scoop out a hole, a pretty shallow one, and pile up some of the big stones around the edges.

The lady thinks this is great. When I look up she presses her hands together and nods her head.

But now we've got to move the dog.

It's less than a metre away from the hole, but I don't want to touch it, not even with her rubber gloves. She doesn't offer them anyway. She's just sitting there, not helping. I realise I've got my water shoes on, so I make myself give the dog a push with the side of my foot. It's heavy, and soft, and even touching it with my shoe is horrible. But it moves.

'Don't kick him!' the lady screams, and she stands up with her hand over her mouth. 'Please, don't kick him.'

'I'm not kicking him,' I say, and I can feel tears coming because I'm doing my best. 'I'm being gentle. I'm just pushing him.' And I have another go, a slower push this time, and she seems calmer. It takes a few pushes to get it to the side of the hole, me watching her all the time, and we both make a face as it sort of half-slides, half-rolls in, making a scrunching sound on the sand and pebbles. Flies are everywhere and I hold my breath because of the smell. But it's over, without disturbing it too much.

I keep watching her as I start putting stones and sand over it, as gently as I can, and she comes to help me put bigger stones on the top. 'I'll find something to mark it,' she says, and she walks off down the path.

She's gone for a while. And I stand there. I stand looking at it – the grave. And I remember when I stood by Dad's grave with my mum, and I knew I shouldn't cry because she was sobbing and shaking and I wanted to be strong, because Dad was gone and now it was just me left to look after her. I had to be the strong one, because Mum was holding tight on to my shoulder, leaning, pressing down, like I was stopping her from falling.

Ever since Dad got ill, she had been holding on to me. We'd been holding on to each other, crying together, trying to keep strong, as every day he got weaker and quieter and sort of smaller. Until we stood at his grave and Mum threw in some soil with a wobbly hand and the stones in the dry dirt made a horrible pattering sound.

And now the lady comes back, with a piece of wood rubbed smooth and clean by the tide, and we put it at the head end of the grave. I bash it in with a big stone and the lady sighs. She holds her gemstone crystal thing in her fingers and her lips move, but I can't hear any words.

Then she says 'Thank you,' and we walk back, and she touches my shoulder very lightly.

That night we have cottage pie and Mum and Mark ask me what I've been doing, so I tell them about the dog.

Mark puts some more Daddies sauce on the edge of his plate and looks up. 'I've seen that when I've been running,' he says. 'It's been on the beach for a couple of weeks, and it's not a dog, it's a fox. It's just an old dead fox that ended up in the harbour and got washed up.'

I finish my tea and go upstairs. Later on Mum tucks me in and asks me if I'm all right. I nod, but I don't open my eyes, and when the door's shut I help myself go to sleep by pretending I'm skimming stones, sending them skipping and spinning over the water, light and fast, flying way out to sea.

A short break

Chrissy watched him come through the high archway and into the room, trench coat draped over one arm, nicely tailored tweed jacket over well-fitting fashionable jeans, shiny tan brogues.

She liked the brogues. Slicked-back grey hair and about the right amount of stubble: glancing at the paintings, but not really looking at them. Looking at the people. The knot of eager tourists with their guide, the family in cagoules and backpacks in town for the day, the pair of earnest art students with sketchbooks. Looking at her, too, as she sat on one of the polished wood benches in front of one of her favourite paintings: Carlo Crivelli's dizzying The Annunciation, with Saint Emidius.

Mostly, though, he was watching the gallery security guard. All the time Chrissy had been looking at Crivelli's vision of the Virgin Mary, zapped by a piercing beam of light from heaven as she prays in her bedroom, the guard had been on a chair at the side of the painting, facing her bench. Now he was up, taking a stroll, nodding at visitors as he passed. Looking at his watch. Thinking about lunch, she guessed.

The guy with the brogues paused in front of a painting near the entrance and she could see him pretending to check it out. Apparently absorbed, he rubbed his chin with a forefinger, revealing a slim leather bracelet of restrained design. But his eyes remained on the guard, who was now going through the archway into the next room of early Renaissance Italian masterpieces. The guy crossed the oak floor and sat down on the bench next to Chrissy's, where a middle-aged couple were studying an unfolded plan of the gallery, the husband weighed down with camera equipment.

'Wait a second, honey,' said the husband, 'let me find my glasses.' He put down an expensive-looking camera lens on the bench and began patting his pockets. Finding his spectacles, he joined his wife in planning their next stop, heads bent over the map.

Chrissy watched the brogues guy place his trench coat on the bench, over the spare lens. Apparently satisfied that the couple were engrossed in their conversation, he slid his hand under the coat, gripped the lens and got up, coat draped over his hand and arm, moving smoothly off the bench and out of the room. Not before giving Chrissy another quick look. And a wink.

The couple on the bench were now arguing about how much time they could spend in the building. Chrissy took one more look at Mary, grabbed her bag and followed the guy with the brogues.

He was in his late forties, she guessed, a bit older than her. He moved quickly through the gallery and out, down the magnificent steps leading on to Trafalgar Square, heading for a bus stop where a double-decker was waiting, engine running. Chrissy put on a spurt of speed and followed him on to it. She caught up with him on the upper deck as they moved off. She sat down beside him and put her bag between her feet.

He glanced over to her and grinned. Wow, that grin.

'Did you see the UFO?' he said.

'What?'

'The UFO. A lot of people reckon that's a UFO he painted in the sky, shooting the Virgin Mary with a laser beam.'

She smiled. 'I think it's meant to be the Holy Spirit.' They were quiet for a while, then she said: 'What are you going to do with it now? The camera lens.'

'I know a guy who shifts this kind of stuff,' he said. 'Thought I'd go and see him this afternoon and see what he says.' His manner was easy and classless and his accent not that different from her own, shaped by her childhood on a Shepherds Bush estate. But there were traces of public school in his voice, hints that betrayed a background he preferred to conceal.

'Nice piece of work,' Chrissy said. 'Very discreet.'

'Not that discreet – you saw me.'

'Well, yes. But I know what to look for.' She paused. Then: 'How come you're talking to me like this? How do you know I'm not police?'

'I realised you'd seen me nick it. It was too late by then. If you were a copper or plainclothes security then you knew I'd done it, I was finished anyway. If you weren't then you were probably in the same game as me.'

A short break

'So is it one of your regular hunting grounds?'

'Not really. I was actually in there because I'm interested in paintings. But it's not bad, you know, for the spur-of-the-moment type of thing. Lots of half-witted tourists not paying attention to their stuff. People are so stupid with their valuables. And if it's on a plate, you take it, don't you?' He shot her a glance. 'But I tend to do more of the confidence stuff – have a bit of fun. That's why I like that painting, the one you were looking at. Did you see old Saint Emidius, in the street, stopping the Archangel Gabriel and distracting him from the job he's supposed to be doing, giving Mary the big news? Did you see what he's carrying with him?'

Chrissy thought back to the Crivelli. 'He's holding a kind of model of some buildings. Like a miniature town.'

'Yeah, he's giving him the sell, pushing some property investment thing. He's saying to the angel: Look at this for an opportunity, I've got it all planned out, here's what it's going to look like. It's some dodgy development deal he's got going.'

'I never thought of it like that.' She was silent for a little while. Then she put out her hand. 'Chrissy,' she said.

'Eddie,' he said, putting out his. That grin again.

'OK,' she said, when they'd shaken. Her mind was made up now. 'Want to go for a drink?'

The bus stopped and they joined a queue of people pushing to get off. Eddie tripped on the bottom step and stumbled on to a man in a business suit. For a second there was a tangle of trench coat, briefcase, umbrella and apologetic gestures.

Then Eddie and Chrissy were off the bus and he had the businessman's wallet in his pocket. That was lunch sorted.

§

Catching herself in the mirror behind the bar, she wasn't too displeased. She wasn't looking her best, but she was glad she always made a point of starting the day looking as smart as she could. Even today, in extreme circumstances. The half-hour she'd spent in the National Gallery ladies' room, as soon as the building opened, had paid off.

By this time there was not much left of their bottle of champagne, courtesy of the business type, and Chrissy was feeling good. A lot better than she had for a long time. Certainly better than earlier today, when she had taken refuge in the gallery as a way of killing time and keeping out of the rain, to avoid depleting any further the small amount of cash she had.

She was giving Eddie a brief account of what had happened. That morning she had walked out on Kevin – out of their flat in Carshalton and out of her old life. All she had now was what she had managed to grab at the time and stuff into her elderly Mazda. The car, parked in a quiet street in Wimbledon, at the end of the District line, was where she was planning to spend the night.

'Kev was up to all kinds of stuff,' she said. 'Nicking, scams, going along on other people's jobs, people smarter than him, to be the muscle – the strong, silent type who just has to stand there being intimidating and persuasive. I know what goes on, and to be honest, I didn't ask too many questions. I enjoyed having the money. I had a crap childhood, always been skint, and I didn't really mind where the dosh came from. But then he crossed a line. He was coming home cut up and bruised – obviously been fighting. He admitted the jobs were getting violent, they were hurting people. I didn't like the violence. But it seemed like he was beginning to get off on it. And then he brought it home – he started on me. That was my cue. I told him: Lay a finger on me again, and I'm off.'

'And you went.'

'Yep, with nowhere to go. Had to. I don't want to end up in hospital.'

Eddie took a sip of champagne and shook his head. 'I hate that. Can't stand blokes who think that's how to get their way, how to react.

'Same goes for how you make your money. I don't mind breaking a few laws to get it, but I don't like it getting physical. Violence is never good.

'Anyway, got to keep my good looks,' he said, smiling, lightening the mood. He raised his glass. 'Here's to letting other people work hard, to having fun and enjoying what matters. Champagne, great art…'

'And decent food,' said Chrissy, raising her glass now. 'Pass me a menu, will you? Let's find a table. I'm bloody starving.'

They both chose lamb cutlets with roasted vegetables. When they were full, finishing off a fine claret of Chrissy's choice, Kevin dabbed his lips with a napkin, sat back and motioned for the bill. 'So you've got a car?' he said.

'Haven't you?'

'I'm between cars at the moment. I tend to borrow them from other people, if you see what I mean, and you can't hang on to them for long, too risky.'

'Well, I've got one. Not much petrol in it, and it's full of my stuff.'

'No problem. Let's go and pick it up. We'll offload this lens on the way – should bring in enough for a tank or two. Come on, let's settle up here and get going, and we can decide where to go from here.'

On the way out, Chrissy caught sight of herself in the bar mirror again. What are you doing? she asked herself. She paused, her hand on the back of a chair, while she considered the question. Hours ago she had been at rock bottom: no money and no hope. A new man was the last thing on her mind. But this guy… no one had made her feel like this for years. She looked at her reflection again. You know what? she thought. I'm going to follow him outside, and I'm going to see what happens.

Eddie was on the street checking the business type's soft calfskin wallet. It was nicely replete, with several credit cards and an impressive amount of cash. They headed for the nearest tube station.

§

And that was how it all got started. After selling the lens and picking up Chrissy's car, Eddie directed her to a large, shabby town house in West Kensington where he got out, asking her to wait. She watched him peer through the front window, pick up a key from under a brick in the front yard and disappear into the building. He was gone for just a few moments, emerging with two large suitcases and a set of golf clubs, closing the front door quietly behind him. He was keen for her to get going.

'Just one thing,' said Chrissy before she put the car into gear.

'Try me.'

'You're single, right? No kids, no ties.'

He nodded. 'OK,' she said, 'so that makes two of us then.' And they were off.

They headed north-west out of London, through market towns and villages where wealth was conspicuous. Deep into the Chiltern Hills, in a village of long driveways and luxury German SUVs, with a golf club on the outskirts, they checked into a smart country hotel.

'Just a short break, is it?' the reception guy said. A sweaty man in his fifties, he had a badge saying 'Leonard'.

'We're looking at houses around here,' said Chrissy, 'aren't we darling?' She smiled at Eddie and touched his arm. Eddie nodded and beamed at Leonard. He patted one of the clubs in his golf bag.

'And playing a few rounds, if I get a chance…'

'Well, we'll have to see, won't we?' said Chrissy, and Eddie looked sheepish. She turned back to Leonard. 'We've really got our hearts set on this area,' she said. 'And the place we saw today, we think it might be the one. Just a few more to see, though, before we make up our minds.'

Leonard was thrilled. 'Well,' he said, 'this is a lovely part of the world. Good luck!'

Chrissy had to admit the golf clubs were a nice touch.

The room had a very comfortable-looking four-poster bed. Chrissy put her bag down and Eddie hung his coat over the back of an armchair. They had ordered champagne up to the room. 'I need a shower,' she said. 'Care to join me?'

'Good idea,' said Eddie, walking over and kissing her. They were nearly late for dinner.

§

They stayed three nights, running up quite a bill. The third night was a Friday, and by the evening the bar was beginning to fill up with local residents, no doubt kicking back after a tough week in the City. Eddie and Chrissy had been exploring the area, almost as if they really were scouting for houses. They came across a stately home with an impressive art collection, though their favourite period was not well represented. The cash from the camera lens and the business guy's wallet served for incidental expenditure, but was starting to run low.

They ate well in the fashionably stripped-back dining room, enjoying the attentions of the staff, who appreciated their generous tips. Chrissy started with the fish: crispy cod cheeks with saag aloo and mango and chilli salsa, while Eddie liked the look of the bubble and squeak with oak smoked bacon. They both went for the char-grilled rib eye steak, vegetables on the side. Chrissy asked the wine waiter for suggestions, and after a short discussion chose two bottles of Alsatian Pinot Noir. 'A good choice,' he said, with a tiny bow.

'You know your stuff,' said Eddie.

'I did a course on wine,' she said. 'Could never afford top quality myself, but I wanted to learn about it.' She took a sip. 'You can go for the priciest one,' she said, 'or you can go for the right one. This was about the third most expensive.'

'Well, here's to the finer things,' he said, raising his glass.

They drank, and she said: 'You're right. You need them. That's why I always used to go to the National

Gallery when things got bad with Kev. And I nearly always ended up in that collection, where we – where I first saw you. Those paintings… the colours. Some of them are so strange, but so beautiful. They lifted me…'

'So what were you planning to do? You know, when you left. You couldn't have carried on sleeping in your car.'

'No, I was trying to think of people whose sofas I could sleep on. But it wasn't a very long list. Kev didn't like me having friends of my own: they had to be "our" friends. Same way he didn't like me earning my own money, being independent. I was supposed to rely on him, the big breadwinner, except I never knew when the bread was going to appear.

'So to be honest with you, I didn't really have a plan. No money stashed away and no way of making any. I've never had a proper job – I've lived off Kev's ill-gotten gains nearly all my life and up to now it's worked out.' She looked at him intently. 'I bet you're thinking twice about going on the road with me, aren't you? A bit of a liability.'

She liked the way he looked at her then, slowly shaking his head. 'No way,' he said. 'I wouldn't be here if I thought that. Anyway, I'm not a great catch myself. You know where I was staying, in West Ken? A friend of a friend's place. It was all right for a while, but I had a bit of a bad run with some business I was in, and it got a bit tricky paying the rent. A week or two more and I would have got thrown out. So you did me a favour…'

The waiter approached for their dessert orders. A dark chocolate délice for her, tarte tatin for him.

Afterwards, relaxed, comfortable with each other, they sat on high stools at the bar and tried a few gins.

She watched Eddie in his element, telling stories, buying drinks for the bar staff and the locals. He wasn't holding back. Soon the music came on, loud.

There was a small dance floor at one end of the large room. 'Come on' said Eddie, draining his glass, sliding off his stool. 'Let's have a boogie.'

She held up her hands and shook her head, smiling. 'No, I'm all right. You go ahead.' And then he was on the floor, in the midst of it, demonstrating some tidy moves. Slapping the local guys on the back, twirling a couple of the women around, doing a passable Michael Jackson moonwalk. She liked the way he still looked over to her now and again, even in the thick of it, his eyes urging her to join in. And eventually, she did. It was a good night.

In the morning it was time to move on. Downstairs at reception, Leonard tapped a few keys and printed out the bill while they sat on a leather sofa opposite the desk and flipped through the papers. Eddie went up to pay, offering one of the business guy's cards. Leonard tapped a few more keys and looked up. 'I'm really sorry sir, but this card's been declined,' he said. 'Do you have another one, perhaps?'

Chrissy could see Eddie thinking. If that card didn't work, none of them would. They would all have been cancelled. And they had booked in under the business type's name, so they could hardly fall back on the other cards, bearing a variety of names, that Eddie had stashed away.

'That can't be right,' he said. 'Could you try again?' Leonard tried again and shook his head. Eddie looked over at Chrissy. 'Some problem with the card,' he said.

Chrissy came up to the desk. 'What do you mean?'

'It's been rejected or something. Some glitch with the bank.'

Leonard looked from one worried face to the other. 'Let me ring them,' said Eddie. 'I'm really sorry. I'll ring them and get it sorted.'

They moved away from the desk to an area by the main door, Eddie pacing up and down doing a great job of acting out a phone conversation with the bank. Every now and again, he would cover up the phone and give her a loud update on what the bank idiots were saying, and she would shake her head and look frustrated.

They went back to Leonard. 'I can't believe this,' said Eddie. 'You know we're buying a house? I got made redundant a few years ago and got a nice pay-off. Got another job straight away and never touched it. All locked away in a savings account. Then, we decided to buy a house, and we need the money for the deposit and a survey and all that. So I transferred the redundancy money into the current account. That one.' He pointed at the card in Leonard's sweaty fingers. 'There's loads in it, the bank can see it in there. But they're saying the transfer hasn't cleared or something so we can't touch the money. And now it's the weekend and they can't do anything.'

'You don't have another card? Another account?' said Leonard.

'Well, no, because we've just got engaged' – Chrissy couldn't help shooting him a glance – 'and we closed our individual accounts, you know, to put our money all together in one place. We thought there'd be more than enough in there, with my redundancy, but now they're saying those funds aren't – 'he turned to Chrissy. 'What's that word they used, darling? I told you the word…

'Accessible?' she said.

'Accessible,' said Eddie. 'It's our money but it's not accessible. Bloody nightmare. I'm so sorry about this, Leonard, it's so embarrassing. But look, it'll be fine on Monday, I'll be here first thing, soon as the banks open, and by then it'll all have gone through. You've got my address and my number.'

Yes, thought Chrissy, good luck with those.

She could see Leonard was buying it, beginning to soften, as Eddie continued his spiel. 'And look,' he said, spreading his arms. Just a bloke asking another bloke for a break, putting it all on the line. 'I'll leave my clubs here as security. Would that work?'

They waited for Leonard to go and talk to someone, and to come back and look stern, while agreeing to the plan. He didn't need the golf clubs, no worries. They left, with more apologies, telling old Leonard he was great, they'd see him on Monday. And then it was on to the next place.

In the car, Chrissy said: 'So, we're engaged now, are we? Good job I've got my mother's old ring on that finger.' And Eddie gave her a big grin. 'I knew you had it,' he said, 'I think that worked. People don't want to spoil a nice story.'

It worked at the next place, a smart independent hotel off the motorway, where they had a free congratulatory bottle of prosecco delivered to their room.

But at their next stop, Eddie declared he liked to vary his tactics – they would use a different plan to get a good meal. Finding the town's best hotel, they entered the lobby, with new arrivals waiting at reception. A family with two kids signed in, got their room key and left. A couple in their 30s, with matching sets of posh luggage, were next. Chrissy sat in an armchair, scrolling through her phone, as Eddie pretended to read the tourist leaflets on the reception counter, getting close and taking in the conversation.

'Got it,' he said, coming back to her. 'Got their name and room number and had a good look at the bloke's signature.' That evening was quieter than the last, but the food was even better. To start: pear, blue cheese and Treviso salad for madame; and ham hock terrine, pickles and sourdough for sir. Then a shared main course: Chateaubriand, seasonal vegetables and potatoes with béarnaise sauce. A nicely aged Barolo, Chrissy's choice again, seemed to do the job.

Eddie got the waiter over, asked for the bill and put the meal on the posh couple's room tab. He drained his glass and raised it to them. 'Cheers,' he said. 'But we did skip dessert.'

They still needed a cash-flow boost. In the next market town, Chrissy stopped at a newsagents to buy a duplicate receipt book with carbon sheets. They each took one half of the town and spent the morning hitting the streets on foot, visiting pubs and signing them up for half-page spots in their prestigious new guide to local hospitality venues, soon to be published. It was a slog, but enough landlords and bar managers were happy enough to cough up the £30 fee for a placement to make it worthwhile.

Chrissy finished first. She sat in a cafe planning an itinerary for the next few days, taking in the sights and some likely opportunities for income generation. She finished one coffee and ordered another, this time with a slice of lemon drizzle cake. 'Nice to treat yourself, isn't it?' said the woman behind the counter.

Yes,' said Chrissy. 'Yes, it is.' She felt a freedom and excitement she had never known before.

They celebrated their haul over lunch in a cool vegan place and discussed what to do that afternoon. 'It's like being on holiday,' said Eddie.

'Better,' said Chrissy, clinking her glass with his. She pointed to a poster for an antiques fair on the wall opposite. 'You fancy a look at that? Might be good for an hour or two.' It was disappointing, apart from one thing that caught her eye: a box of vintage costume jewellery, including a dozen rings encrusted with fake gems and of varying degrees of ugliness. She rummaged in the box until she had all the rings and carried out a brisk negotiation with the dealer. They paid a little over the odds for them, but Chrissy didn't mind. She knew they would come handy.

§

Next town, next job. And Chrissy was calling the shots on this one.

It took a while to find the right pub, with just the right level of seediness. Once they'd located a likely target, they parked a few streets away. She looked up the pub's number on her phone and dialled. She put the phone to her ear, while in the other hand she held up one of the rings from the antiques fair, bearing a large faux emerald surrounded by small, simulated diamonds.

'Yeah, hello, White Hart.' A male voice, not too polite. Drinkers laughing in the background.

'Hello, yes, I'm really sorry to bother you, I'm just phoning round a few places to see if anyone's had a ring handed in?'

'A ring? When?'

'Well, I was out last night and I lost it, and I'm just ringing round where we went, you know, because last night was the last time I saw it. I thought someone might have handed it in.'

'Hang on.' Muffled steps, a conversation out of earshot. 'No, sorry love. Nothing here. OK?' He went to hang up.

'No, hang on, can I just say…? If anyone does hand it in, there's a reward, because it's got a lot of sentimental value for me, for my family. I mean, it's worth a bit, because it's got diamonds and an emerald, so I was thinking of a reward around £500. But mainly it's the sentimental value. We just need people's help to find it.'

A change of tone at the other end. '£500? OK, I understand. I can see if it turns up. So do you want to give me a number or something, so I can let you know?'

'Sure,' said Chrissy, feeling it coming together, giving a thumbs-up to Eddie next to her in the car. She made up a mobile number. 'Thanks a lot. My name's Kathy. Let me know, I appreciate it. Bye…'

'Yeah, OK Kathy, will do. Hope you find it. Bye now.'

Chrissy ended the call and put her phone down. 'I

think I know what's coming,' said Eddie. 'We wait until tonight, and I go round there with the ring, and…

'You go up to the barman and tell him you just found it in the car park or somewhere. He'll have searched every inch of the pub by then, so you'll need to think of somewhere outside where I could have dropped it.'

'Excellent,' he said, grinning. 'I know this one, it's a classic.'

'Yeah, Kev used to say the East End guys swore by it in the old days. He'd never have been able to pull it off though. He's not smart enough, for a start. And I don't think he's got the balls.'

§

They checked into a smart little B&B, and later that night drove back to the side street near the White Hart. Eddie got out and she watched him walk down the street, a lot scruffier than usual, his hands stuffed into the pockets of a Harrington jacket, striding along in Adidas trainers. Looking the part. Less than 20 minutes later he was back, seeming very pleased with himself and patting his inside jacket pocket.

She listened as she drove back to the B&B, enjoying the story. 'I took my time,' he said. 'I got a pint and sat at the bar and waited until he had no one to serve and was just standing there.

'I get his attention and he comes over, asks me if I want another one lined up. I say no, I was just wondering if anyone in here had lost a ring. You should have seen his eyes light up. He comes in close and I pull it out of my pocket. "I found it in the car park," I say, "just now. Looks expensive." He squints at it for a bit and then puts his hand out.

'"Cheers mate," he says. "Bloke who comes in here has been looking for that. His missus lost it and I promised to phone them if it turned up. They'll be so chuffed. Very good of you to hand it in."

'I look a bit reluctant. I say, on the other hand, he could give me the bloke's number, and I could arrange to give it to them.'

She looked over to see Eddie grinning, remembering the barman's reaction. 'He didn't like that idea much. According to him, the bloke's a really good friend, and he wants to hand it over personally. I give him a hard look and say: "Look mate, are you being straight with me?" He gets all defensive, saying he doesn't know what I'm getting at, so I ask him point-blank if there's a reward.

'He says yes, but he's not telling me what it is or giving me the phone number. What he is happy to do, is give me £100 if I hand over the ring, for my trouble. I say no way, I found it, and it must be worth something. So what about £300? He comes back with £200, and in the end I settle for £250. Can't say fairer than that.'

Eddie patted his pocket again. 'It came straight out of the till, in tenners. Nice little job.'

'You think he'll go for the reward, or try and sell it first?'

'Oh, I'm pretty sure he'll try and sell it,' said Eddie. 'He bought me a Scotch.'

And that's how it was, for a week. And then another week, and a third. Hitting the road most mornings, putting a suitable distance between them and their last target. The English countryside flashing by, soundtracked by Chrissy's limited playlist: either Earth, Wind and Fire or Mozart.

They'd arrive somewhere, decide on a plan and split the proceeds. Sometimes it was the redundancy money thing, sometimes the eavesdropping trick. Sometimes they just did a runner. If they got short of cash then there was the ring scam, or the pub directory con. Or, of course, Eddie might just bump into someone.

§

In a central Oxford hotel, a monumental piece of Victorian Gothic with a very 21st century level of comfort, Chrissy lay in a deep bath thinking about what a team she and Eddie had turned out to be, and what a run they'd had so far. There had been some tricky moments – a close call or two, a few times when only a bit of fast talking had saved them. But here they were, in a place she had always dreamed of visiting, and they had acquired enough money to relax and behave like ordinary tourists for a while. The hotel bill was a problem for another day. They would think of something.

Soon they would go down for cocktails and a meal, check out the wine list. And in the morning they would explore the historic city together. This man was starting to mean a lot to her, and she was happier than at any time in her life.

It was a lot warmer the next day, and she felt good in a new floral top and pale jeans, with heels low enough to be comfortable as they toured the colleges and took in the glorious architecture. A new, sharper hairstyle, courtesy of an upmarket salon en route, showed off her petite features.

She was aware of Eddie watching her as they walked through Christ Church Meadow along the river, holding hands. He seemed aware that although she was happy, the future loomed in her thoughts. 'Lovely, isn't it?' she said. 'Not a patch on Carshalton, of course, but not bad.'

'Yes, it's beautiful,' Eddie said. A pause, then: 'Are you OK?'

'I was just thinking… a few weeks ago I was facing a night sleeping in my car, terrified about what would happen next, with my money running out. And now we're having this amazing time, staying at lovely hotels, taking in these unbelievable views and buildings… '

'But…'

'What?'

'You're going to say: "But…" and tell me it's not going to last. The whole Bonnie and Clyde thing.'

'Well, it's not, is it? I can't believe some of the stuff we've got away with. I think we're a good team, we're careful and we're pretty successful. But these days there's computer records and CCTV and all that… and one day we'll run out of luck. They'll catch up with us sooner or later and it'll all be over. '

He looked at her, put his hands on her shoulders, waiting for her to look him in the eye. He kissed her. 'Yes,' he said, 'it'll all be over. Might be today, might be a long time yet. But are you enjoying it?'

'Yes, of course I am.'

'So why not keep going?'

She was quiet for a while. Then she said: 'You know what I thought when we first got together?'

'What?'

'I thought, I've lived off a small-time criminal most of my life, I know how it all works, and I bet I can do a better job myself. I can do it with a bit more of this' – she tapped her temple – 'and definitely with a lot more style. And I've found a partner with just the right qualities…'

'I'm flattered,' he said.

'But now I'm thinking, maybe we should quit while we're ahead.'

'Or, try another part of the country, new territory, see how it goes…'

She thought about it. 'I don't know. I think the first thing is, we should make the most of today, and then tomorrow we need to get out of the area. Then we can figure out what we're going to do in the future.'

They walked further. Then he stopped, and said: 'Listen, Chrissy.' She looked at him. 'I don't want you to get the wrong idea.'

'What do you mean?'

'I mean, about me. The future. I don't want you to have any illusions. I've never been much good at planning, thinking about what's next. I guess that's why I haven't done that much with my life. I've never had goals. Even the con stuff. I can do it, but I've been happier just going with the flow. To be honest, I've been pretty lazy: scrounging off friends, doing the whole Wherever I Lay my Hat thing. I've disappointed a lot of people, got into a lot of trouble. These last few weeks, with you… I've really raised my game. But what I'm saying is: I don't want you thinking I'm something I'm not.'

Chrissy said nothing for a while. Then: 'OK. Well, I haven't made a lot of great choices either, in my life. I'm not sure I'm such a great bet.'

They walked on for a while, until she broke the silence. 'That pub by the old city walls,' she said, 'the famous one that's hidden down a little passageway. Let's see if we can find that.'

They had lunch there, traditional steak pie and real ale, at a courtyard table in the shadow of a 15th century bell tower. A few more colleges followed, and a few more pubs. By late afternoon they were in the Ashmolean Museum, in front of Uccello's The Hunt in the Forest. It was one of the most popular sights in the museum, attracting a stream of tourists who stopped, glanced at it for a few moments and then shuffled on. Chrissy and Eddie stood before it, unmoving, saying nothing: mute obstructions to the flow of visitors threading their way through the display cabinets.

They both felt the strange power of the scene: an endless woodland at night, its ancient peace turned to chaos by men on horseback and on foot, baying dogs on the loose. The hunters driving on through the trees, hungry for a kill: closing in on a herd of deer which scatters in terror. Uccello had used perspective so dramatically that Chrissy felt she was being dragged into the scene, pulled into the depths of the forest, towards an inevitable end.

She looked over to Eddie and waited for him to turn and meet her gaze. 'Come on,' she said, breaking the spell. 'I need to get outside.'

He puffed out his cheeks. 'Yes, you're right. It's a

bit claustrophobic in here. Let's get some fresh air.' He brightened. 'Look, tell you what – why don't we have a picnic? Let's get some nibbles together, a few treats, a nice bottle of something. I know a place we can have it.'

She agreed. They could do anything they wanted. A picnic, in the sunshine, was just what they needed.

§

Worcester College gardens, by the lake. They explored the grounds for a while, swinging their bags of picnic goodies, nodding to students passing by and other strolling couples enjoying the sunshine. Then they found a spot by the water, ate freshly made sandwiches and drank champagne out of plastic cups.

'Where next?' said Chrissy.

'You're joking, aren't you?' said Eddie. 'I can't move. Too much food, too much booze…'

'But there's still places to see. Colleges, museums… I've never been anywhere like this before.'

'OK,' said Eddie, putting his hands behind his head and lying back on the grass. 'You decide. Wake me up when it's time to go.'

Chrissy took out her phone and began flicking through pages of local information. Several minutes passed as she bent over the screen, shielding it from the sun. Then one hand flew to her mouth. Reaching over to Eddie, she knocked over her champagne and it trickled into the grass.

'Eddie,' she said. It was almost a whisper. 'Eddie, look at this.'

He got up on one elbow, squinting into the sunlight.

'What's the matter?'

'This,' she said. 'Look. It's all over.' She watched his face change as he read the page from the *Oxford Mail* headlined 'Con couple's trail of trickery', with a still taken from CCTV footage at one of their country hotel stops. There was Eddie, with his grin and his stubble. And there, with her new haircut and her hand on his arm, was she.

'Well,' he said eventually. 'That's a shame. I was enjoying being back.' She heard a flat finality in his voice that had never been there before.

'What are you talking about?'

'Here,' he said, as she stared at him. 'The college. I was here for a couple of years, studying English. Until I screwed it all up, of course, and got chucked out.'

'You never told me.'

'I didn't tell you a lot of things. I didn't tell you I'd been inside, did I?'

'No,' she said.

'Well, I have. I've done my fair share of time – all my own fault, I admit it – and I'll tell you one thing, I do not want to go back.' He got up and draped his trench coat over his arm. 'Time for me to get going. Sorry.'

He lunged for her bag, and as she got to her feet to try to stop him, he found her car key and took two steps back. 'Chrissy, I tried to tell you. I tried to warn you – not to trust me. We had a good time – it was brilliant. But like you said, it's all over now. I can move faster on my own.'

'Wait,' she said, eyes flashing. 'Just wait a second.' He turned, reluctantly. 'See this?' she said, holding up her phone again. 'Know what this is?'

He looked closer. A business class booking to Paris on

the Eurostar. 'OK,' he said. 'Nice work. Just for one?'

'Just me, one way. I've always wanted to go to the Louvre, walk on the Left Bank, try those restaurants. I bought this as soon as we got some money together…

She broke off as he registered surprise. 'Yes, that's right, I've had it for ages,' she said. She jabbed a finger at him, 'But you know what? I had no intention of using it. It was my insurance, just in case you did something like this. In case you were just a spineless, selfish bastard like every other bloke I've known. So you can have the car, and see how far you get. I'm going to Paris. Now – get lost.'

He dropped her bag, pocketed the car key and was gone. Chrissy scooped her things together, checked the location of the rail station on her phone, and strode out of the college grounds and into the street. She had to get on a train to London and then out of the country as soon as she could. She knew going back to the hotel was out of the question: their pictures would have been shared around every hospitality business in the area.

She walked grimly on through the city, oblivious to the architecture that had entranced her hours earlier. The champagne buzz was gone. She was on her own, just as she had been when she walked out on Kev, just as she had been many times before. She would survive. She bought a ticket to London and sat on the platform, tapping her foot as the minutes on the overhead display ticked down.

A young guy wearing headphones sat beside her and she pulled her bag closer, shrinking into the seat. She took out her phone, seeking distraction, but then turned it off. What if her location was being tracked? The young guy took a call and got up, pacing the platform as he talked.

A short break

The time ticked by on the electronic display. The train to Paddington was now five minutes away. She stared at her shoes.

And then someone else sat down beside her.

She saw the brogues, then the trench coat over his arm. She stood up quickly, went to walk down the platform, but he took hold of her wrist. She knew it would not be good to make a scene. 'Let go of me,' she hissed. 'Now.'

'OK,' he said, releasing her. 'But Chrissy, please. Please sit down. I don't want to split up. I changed my mind.'

'And what about me? I haven't changed mine. Same plan as far as I'm concerned. I'm going to Paris.'

'I know,' he said. 'I'm sorry. I never got as far as the car. I knew I wanted to be with you. I knew – '

'Shut up,' she said.

'Please, Chrissy, just hear me out.'

'No, shut up. Be quiet. Can you hear that?' It was getting louder. Police sirens. The Paddington train was now three minutes away. 'They must have our picture in the ticket office too,' she said. 'That's it, then. It really is all over now. You should have taken the car, shouldn't you? You might have had a chance.'

'No Chrissy, I shouldn't.' He paused. The sirens had stopped. 'Look, he said, 'quickly. Take your mother's ring off.'

'What?'

'You mother's old ring. Take it off.'

Staring at him in disbelief, she did what he asked. The train was now two minutes away, and she could see a couple of police officers coming along the platform towards them, one talking into his radio.

'Put this on instead,' Eddie said, pulling back his trench coat to show, in his palm, the least garish of the vintage rings they had bought from the antiques fair. 'Something to remember me by.' A single faux diamond did its best to sparkle in the early evening light.

The overhead display ticked over to show one remaining minute, as the officers made their way towards them, pushing past the people now lining the platform, the train visible in the distance.

They were not getting on it. They were not going to Paris. Not for a while, anyway. There was no time to talk things over, no time to think. She stared at Eddie and shook her head.

'You've got some front,' she said.

Then he got up, ready, and Chrissy stood up next to him. She put the ring on her finger and waited.

The cloud forest

Westhampton Museum, England, October 2018

Matt winced as the caretaker's big hand came down on the desk, slap, sending a pair of forceps tinkling to the floor and dozens of tiny pins cascading from their box.

'Got it,' said Terry, picking up the broken fly by a wing. 'I'd say bluebottle, but you're the expert.'

Matt checked his stereo microscope and the tray of tropical beetles he had been working on. Though jarred and rattled they were intact.

He turned to the crushed insect offered for his inspection between a fat finger and thumb. 'Yes,' he said, 'you're probably right. Not sure which species. A bit difficult to tell now, of course.'

'Well, you don't want it in here, do you?' said Terry. 'Not with all your rare specimens and that. I thought you had to be careful with pests getting in, chomping their way through everything.'

'No, no, you're absolutely right.' Matt managed a weak smile. 'Thanks. But I'd probably have caught it and let it out of a window.'

Terry looked around the room, in the museum basement. Blank walls, rows of specimen cabinets, a couple of tables with laptops and strange, delicate tools. No natural light. 'You mean, you'd chase a fly around with a net or something until you got it, then go all the way upstairs to a window and let it go?'

'Well, I'd probably take a quick look at it to check what it was, then pop it in a specimen tube. Take it upstairs next time I went.'

Terry shook his head and sighed, rolling his eyes. The academic staff were familiar with this you-boffins-are-crazy routine. 'So,' he said, 'you're happy to have all these dead bugs here, sitting in trays with pins through them, but you don't want to kill one bluebottle.'

'Well, most of these date back to forty, fifty, a hundred years ago. Longer, some of them, and I didn't collect them. I hardly ever kill anything these days, and I don't think you should, unless you really have to. But sometimes you do, so you can study the specimen, and keep it as a record of that species, and help science make progress. One lost individual makes no difference to an insect population. Think about how many bugs get killed and eaten by a single blue tit in a day, or splattered on a windscreen.'

Actually, that was a bad example. Thanks to a host of human crimes against the planet, a bug-spattered car was becoming more and more a thing of the past.

Terry was talkative: the end of the day, his duties finished. 'So, I heard you're working on this new collection, the really big one, from the university?'

'Yep. It's a massive piece of work. Should be cracking on with it really...'

Terry continued anyway. 'They reckon it's amazing – stuff from all over the world. Rainforests and jungles.'

'Well, yes. It's pretty incredible. For a small museum like this, in a small town, to get a collection like this – it's unbelievable. But obviously, it's a full-time job getting it all catalogued and sorted.'

'So, I was wondering: can I see it?'

'What?'

'You know, the star attraction. Haven't we got some kind of cricket thing, the only one in the world?'

'Bush cricket,' said Matt, 'Or a katydid, which is the term most people outside Britain tend to use. This one's called *Pterochroza linwoodi*.'

'Yeah, whatever,' said Terry. 'To be honest, no offence to your job and everything, but bugs and beetles... ' he shuddered. 'They give me the creeps, especially with the pins through them. But my boy – he's seven – he's absolutely mad on science. He saw your cricket thing online, and he knows I work here. He said, could I take a picture. I said I'd ask.'

Matt went over to the cabinet of specimens from Costa Rica's Cartago province, and slid out a tray of katydids, large relatives of grasshoppers with long antennae – their wings and bodies evolved to mimic the plants of their natural habitat, sometimes in extraordinary detail, as a means of evading predators. Now they sat pinned in neat rows behind glass. He put the tray on his desk.

'Wow,' said Terry, pulling out his phone. It was obvious

which one was the prize specimen. It took centre stage in the tray, surrounded by far smaller and less spectacular cousins: two pairs of iridescent wings spread out against the white lining of the case, spiny legs arranged symmetrically, spread-eagled under the basement strip lights.

'The colours fade after death,' said Matt. 'Imagine what it looked like when it was alive.'

§

From *Entomological Travels in Central America*, by Rev Nathaniel Korner, 1893

On each of the hind-wings, a large vivid central eye spot, bright vermilion, surrounded by a thick ultramarine ring and then a thinner one of acid yellow. The background burnt orange, with highlights of pure white. The upper abdomen striped and stippled with a rainbow of colours, fading into the background green of the creature's body. And all these colours invisible, hidden by the dull but impressively camouflaged fore-wings, until the animal leaps into the air and takes flight. On the wing its large size is impressive – approaching that of a small bird – yet it is surprisingly graceful. Once the animal has come to rest in a place of safety, the fore-wings immediately close and the intense colouration of this remarkable insect is a secret once more, as it blends into the tropical foliage with ease. The creature now resembles a leaf – browning at the edges, mottled with incipient decay, veined and nibbled like the leaves of the lush shrubs on which it spends its life – until those extraordinary false eyes are needed once more, to terrify a monkey or raccoon or coatimundi, or indeed a curious human being, in which case they open in an instant and flash in the face of the unsuspecting intruder, startling it long enough for this most singular of God's creatures to make its escape. And so it will live another day, a dazzling spark of paradise in this remote corner of the planet; a bejewelled treasure whose glories are hidden from all but its Creator, and those who happen to glimpse its beauty for a fleeting, rapturous moment.

§

Tapanti National Park, Costa Rica, July 1987

It was noon now, and they were ascending towards the cloud forest, following an ill-defined hunting trail up the densely vegetated hillside, the Orosi River far below them. As soon as they had left the biological research station and crossed the river on a rusty suspension bridge, the landscape had burst into life: birds and butterflies bringing flashes of impossible colour to even the densest areas of forest. Toucans clattered through the upper branches, croaking and braying, as the two men sweated and climbed. This area of Cartago province, recently declared a national park, was the wettest place in the country, and for British scientists helping to survey its fauna, the constantly damp and humid conditions could be punishing. But at least, today, it wasn't raining.

Dennis stopped, resting a hand on a mossy trunk, waiting for Doug. He took a swig from his water bottle and looked down the valley, a waterfall visible far in the distance. A column of ants marched up and down the tree. He got out a specimen tube and scooped a couple into it. He sighed. He could just have collected a species new to science. Every other tube in his backpack could contain a new species. They could probably go home now and have enough material for a dozen research papers. But he needed to find what he was really here for. He needed to get up higher.

Only, where the hell was Doug? Obviously distracted once again, probably not even by an insect, but by a bird or an orchid or the tracks of some kind of mammal. Holding them back. 'Doug!' he yelled down the track. 'Dougie, come on. There's a way to go yet. You know we need to climb a bit more.'

He turned to go back, to find him. And then, there he was, Douglas Linwood, the best PhD student of his generation, striding up the path, Nikon in hand, wearing a lurid rock-band T-shirt and a necklace of rainbow-coloured beads on a leather cord, a recent acquisition from a local market. Doug held up the camera up with a grin. 'Think I saw a quetzal back there, sorry. Looked like one to me, anyway. Incredible bird. Think I got a couple of shots.' He paused, seeing Dennis's expression. 'We doing all right for time?'

Dennis closed his eyes briefly. 'Doug, you know we've got to go up a bit further. I know this is a fantastic place, I know there's so much to see. I'm not blind. We'd all love to spend our time just exploring. But at the end of the day this is work, for God's sake…'

Doug rummaged in his backpack, unwrapped a pack of local cookies and offered one. Dennis shook his head.

Doug shrugged and bit into it. 'Seen that waterfall over there?' he said. 'Wow.'

'Yes, I've seen it. Great. But we need to keep going or it'll be time to turn back – and that'll be another day gone. We've only got one left, if you remember.'

'Yes, I know. It's just…' He looked at Dennis. 'Are you sure this is the best plan?'

'Doug, please, we talked about this. I thought we'd agreed. You've read Korner, same as I have. You've seen his illustrations. Does this look like the habitat in those drawings? No. We think we're in the right kind of area, but have we been climbing for as long as he says he did? No. We need the tree canopy to be lower than this, I think. The vegetation needs to be a bit sparser. That's the most likely kind of habitat we're going to find it in, if we ever do.'

Doug chewed for a while, swallowed. 'OK, OK. I understand where you're coming from,' he said. 'All I'm saying is, you're going on the evidence of one guy, nearly a hundred years ago. An amateur, however good he was, who didn't take a specimen or leave us any field notes. My guess is he catches it, manages to get a reasonable look at it, and maybe makes some sketches in the field– no trace of them now. But he's all excited, and before he can collect it, it gives him the slip and hops off into the forest again. And what we have now is a book of reminiscences, which he writes when he gets home to Chattanooga or wherever.

'I just don't know how reliable he is. And we could be projecting too much from his evidence. He says his specimen was active during the day, but most katydids are nocturnal. God knows, it's hard enough to sleep in this place with them all chirping. For all we know, he could just have disturbed it and assumed it was out and about during the day. We might have a much better chance with a night search.

'And we're not a hundred percent sure whether, as a species, it really does favour these higher elevations. When he found it, it could have been a one-off, an outlier.' He pointed down the valley. 'For all we know there could be a decent population back there.'

Dennis took his hat off, ran his fingers through damp hair. 'Yes, but we've been through this. You're right: the evidence is hardly conclusive, but it's all we've got and we have to give it a shot. Korner is the only person to have seen one…

Doug raised his eyebrows. 'The only person? You sure? What about the local people, over a few thousand years?'

'OK, point taken. He's the only naturalist to have described one. So we have to trust him and follow his lead, at least to start with. And again, you keep going back to the local people. But you've heard the same as me. Stories, anecdotal stuff. They could be referring to any number of species. None of them has specific, proven knowledge of this particular animal. Or are you telling me you got some amazing new information in the bar last night?'

It was hotter now, and the throbbing hum of the cicadas seemed louder, more relentless – as much a property of the air as the oppressive humidity. A bright green basilisk lizard skittered off a leaf the size of a golfing umbrella, where it had been sunbathing. Birds, the names of which they would never know, chattered and screamed, deep in the forest. Somewhere, a jaguar would be dozing, waiting for the sun to go down.

Doug stopped chewing and jabbed the cookie at Dennis. 'OK, Professor Johnson,' he said with mock deference, 'I like to hang out in the bar in the evening, when I've been working hard all day. Are you saying that's a problem?'

Dennis held his hands up. 'No, of course not, I was just…'

'Well, how I relax is up to me. And yes, I know what we're here for. You don't need to tell me how to do my job. We're going to find this thing, and I'll bet you I'm the one who spots it first. You need to relax a bit, you know? Use your imagination, tune into this place a bit. Widen your vision. You'll see nothing with those blinkers on, fretting about getting the job done.'

Doug, the one with all the talent, and the temper. Dennis ignored the outburst. Halfway up a hillside in Central America was not the place for a lecture about respecting seniority.

But the younger man did need a reminder about accountability. 'What about if we don't find it?' Dennis said. 'What then? If we go home with all the grant money spent and nothing to show for it, whose arse is going to be on the line?'

Doug rolled his eyes, resuming his cookie.

'Mine,' said Dennis. 'You got your place on this trip fair and square. Absolutely the right choice. The best field entomologist I've seen come through in years. I value your opinion. But it won't be you facing the music if we don't come back with the goods. We have to follow Korner's lead, demonstrate that we tried to build on his work, before we turn to something else. It's my department and my reputation, and…'

He stopped talking and followed Doug's gaze. A shimmering metallic-green hummingbird – a flash of indigo on its head, turquoise at its throat, wing feathers a deep purple-grey – was feeding from a bright red flower at the side of the trail. They watched it hover, take its fill of nectar, then dart into the bushes.

Dennis got out a handkerchief and wiped his forehead. He took another drink. 'OK, full and frank discussion. Thanks a lot. But this is the best plan we've got for now. Are you coming?'

Doug shrugged, nodded. 'You're the boss.'

'Right then,' said Dennis. 'Then let's get going. I think we've got another hour or two and then we should be high enough to start looking.'

§

Westhampton Museum, October 2018

Matt was finally alone, with a thousand dead insects. The silence in the basement was broken only by the clicking of his keyboard and the ticks and whirs of the system maintaining the room's protective atmosphere.

He had never had a job of this magnitude. Each tray of specimens had to be minutely examined for pests or degradation. Legs might have to be glued back on, corroded pins replaced. The information on the labels, two of which accompanied each creature, had to be checked and updated if necessary, in line with changes in classification. Another label, with the museum's own catalogue numbers, had to be attached. And then the data had to be transcribed on to an online database, along with a high-resolution image of the specimen. Laborious, but fascinating.

Despite its value, the Johnson Collection had not been looked after in recent years – a victim of cutbacks, complacency and shifting academic priorities. Now it was in his care. He was the custodian of a life's work, handling creatures that had once clambered, flown or crawled in some of the world's most remote and biologically-rich locations. All collected by, or under the direct supervision of, one of the late 20th century's most eminent entomologists, a former head of department at the university.

It was fitting that the collection bore Johnson's name. But there was a small inconsistency that bothered Matt, and it nagged at him again as he got up from his desk and carried the tray containing *Pterochroza linwoodi* back to its cabinet. The labelling next to it, following standard practice, listed Johnson as collector of the creature in the wild, and as the authority who had determined the species. So why had this unique specimen, lauded in professional journals and popular science texts alike, not been named after the man who had brought it back to his university, described and classified it, and announced it to his astonished peers around the world?

Matt slid the tray back in. *Linwoodi*, said the species name, in neat indelible characters. But who, he wondered, was Linwood?

His phone was ringing.

'Hi,' said Helen. 'Just checking what your plans are. You know it's 7.30…'

'Is it? Oh God, sorry. Got a lot to do here, and people have been interrupting me all day.'

'You said you were going to cook tonight. I bought what you said, it's all here waiting. Do you want me to start getting it ready?'

'No, I said I'd do it. I will, sorry. Just got to pack up here then I'll be home. OK?'

'OK, see you later.'

'Love you,' he told his wife. But it seemed she had already hung up.

§

Tapanti National Park, July 1987

They were higher now, and the air was denser and even more laden with moisture. The forest was thinner, the trees not so majestic, but it was no less rich in plant and animal life. Pink, yellow and orange bromeliads set the trail ablaze with their blooms – exploding out of the undergrowth in great splashes of colour. White-faced capuchin monkeys were nearby, judging by the sharp barks and squeaks reaching them from the denser stands of trees. The two men swept foliage with their nets and beat branches with sticks, gathering scores of creatures on the trays they held underneath. Their specimen tubes were now full of astonishing insects – neon red-and-blue spotted leafhoppers, clear-winged moths with metallic bodies and dazzling yellow stripes, weevils like polished gems with glowing orange bands. A dozen or so typical katydids, some with flashes of colour and iridescent legs, others indistinguishable from a leaf or clump of lichen.

They worked one side of the track, moved on to the other. Then they walked onwards, higher still, and repeated the process. They were sodden with perspiration and exhausted by the uneven path, at turns muddy and covered with rocks.

Clumping along the trail in dull khaki, Dennis felt he was blending into the forest. It was seducing him, absorbing him. It was offering him its incidental baubles, its casual delights. But not the gift he wanted most of all.

And then it was time to turn back. 'OK Doug,' he said. 'Let's call it a day.' It was difficult to concede defeat, today at least.

'Sure. I think we've given this site a good going over. We got some great stuff, don't you think? Like that weevil. I'm not sure I've seen that in the literature.'

'No, you could be right.'

'Disappointing not to get what you came for, though.'

'Well, we've got tomorrow. Maybe, if we take that left-hand turn back there, we'll strike it lucky. I can't believe this thing's requirements are that different from all the other species we've seen. We must come across one sooner or later.'

'Sure, we could still find it,' said Doug. A pause. He kicked a root on the path. 'Earlier on, you know, when we had a bit of a... discussion. I just wanted to say, uh... sorry. If I went a bit over the top.'

'Likewise, Dougie,' said Dennis. 'No problem. But... '

'What?'

'Up to you, what you do tonight, but first we need to sort out what we got today, OK? Get things ID'd if we can and packaged up for the trip back. There are too many for me to do on my own.'

Doug nodded, and they made their way back down to the valley. It was raining.

§

That night they worked on the specimens they had collected during the day, then ate with expedition colleagues in the communal dining hall. Dennis watched Doug and the younger team members congregate at one end of the long table, laughing and recounting the excitements of the day. Most had never been out of Europe before. Some had never left the UK. This trip – to this lush environment, where life in all its forms was so abundant – was transformative for them.

Two decades ago, had he been like these students? On his first foreign expedition, had he been wide-eyed and open to fresh experiences, inspired by new landscapes and exotic habitats, or had he been too focused on the job in hand, the immediate task before him – however absorbing and stimulating that task had been? The work always had to be done. The data had to be gathered. But did he allow enough room in his mind, in his heart, for the unexpected and the unsought-for?

Dennis ate opposite John Cargill, an amphibian specialist heading a survey of the area's myriad species of frog. 'So,' he said, pointing his fork at Dennis, 'found your beastie yet?' The quest for the elusive katydid had inspired a mixture of mirth and admiration from colleagues.

'Not yet. We're going to have another try tomorrow, at a different site. Knowing my luck, Doug will probably find it before me.'

'That's Doug Linwood, right?'

'Yes, really talented guy, but like a lot of the younger ones... you know, they're so excited by the wealth of fauna here. They're like kids in a sweet shop. It can be hard to get them to focus.'

'But they say he's one to watch, that he'll really make a name for himself one day.'

'Oh yes,' said Dennis. 'Once he's got something in his sights, he's formidable.'

'And I hear he's building a reputation for himself already, in another specialism.' Dennis looked up, puzzled. He didn't follow.

'With the ladies,' said Cargill, with a grin.

'Ah, well, I'm not exactly plugged into the gossip,' said Dennis, 'but I'm sure you're right.' He smiled. 'I'm aware he's had a certain degree of success in that area.'

Cargill shook his head slowly. 'They're amazing,' he said, 'some of these kids. I mean, he's a good-looking guy, women love him, and on top of that he's got a brilliant mind – am I right?'

'Oh yes, remarkable.'

'And, he's one of the lads too. I've watched him drink half of them under the table, and then you see him at the crack of dawn, fresh as a daisy, loading up his kit and heading off for another day's collecting.'

'Yes,' said Dennis. 'It's a long time since I had that kind of energy. If I ever did.'

'Yep,' Cargill said, and shrugged. 'Well, we'd better keep our strength up, I guess, or they're going to leave us behind. Don't know about you, but I'm starving.' And he turned his attention back to his rice and beans.

Finishing his meal, Dennis watched the younger group get up, dump their food trays in a stack and move off noisily, no doubt heading for one of the few bars in the small town nearby. Some of the senior members of the team, around his own age, were clearly going with them.

Cargill was standing up, tray in hand. 'Coming into town?'

'No,' said Dennis. 'Thanks, but I've got stuff to do here. Looks like the rain's stopped, so I think I'll set up the moth trap again.'

'Again?'

'Well, you never know what'll turn up, and we're nearly out of time here…'

'OK.' Cargill shrugged. 'See you later then.'

'Yeah, see you tomorrow.'

Dennis hauled his kit down the trail, away from the research station, until he was surrounded by vegetation and there was no glimpse of artificial light. He unfolded a camping chair and set up his trap: a powerful light source and a white sheet suspended from a branch. And then he waited.

Moths immediately began to arrive – landing on the sheet, on his head and on his arms. From tiny fingernail-sized specimens to the giant White Witch moth, which had a wingspan of almost a quarter of a metre. A large metallic gold beetle settled in the centre of the sheet and remained still, unaffected by the whirring of dozens of wings. Small katydids came and went, as the songs of their relatives in the forest grew louder and louder.

Perhaps Doug was right, he thought. Perhaps we should do a night search. His mind wandered as he gazed at the growing swarm of insects. He thought of his wife Linda, alone back home, and wondered what the time was in England. Being a head teacher at a secondary school meant she, too, worked long hours. They enjoyed the quietness of their time together, and shared a tender familiarity that was not quite love.

They had, eventually, learned to accept that they could not have children. He wondered whether her job was compensation for her in some way. He wondered whether his own job, working with so many young people, was likewise a comfort for him. Had they lost themselves in work, and lost each other? He thought of Doug. Did he cut him too much slack, ignore his outbursts, because he was a brilliant and invaluable colleague, or because he thought of him in some ways as a son?

He dozed off. When he woke, the sheet was thick with moths and other flying insects. Small patches of cloth were visible amongst the mass of living things clinging to the fabric. He got up, stretched, and began to gather the most interesting specimens. He could not hope to collect anything but a small fraction of the creatures that had visited him tonight.

§

The next day he set out again with Doug, across the river and up the old hunting route, to explore the other branch of the trail. Beating and sweeping again produced fascinating finds, but not the fabled katydid. Nor did it seem to be hiding in furled leaves, or in the dense hearts of bromeliads. Drained, hot and frustrated, they called off the hunt early and went back to the research station. Tomorrow they would leave.

'Look,' said Dennis as they crossed the bridge back to their base. 'I was thinking about what you said yesterday, about trying a nocturnal search. We can rest up now, then go straight out after we've eaten. Or…' he looked at Doug, 'are you going into town for the last night?'

Doug scratched the back of his neck. 'No,' he said eventually. 'You're right. We should give it a shot. I can have a couple of beers with the guys before we eat, anyway.'

'OK,' said Dennis. 'Listen, I appreciate it.'

'No problem. I told you I was going to find it. See you later.'

During a night search, katydids would announce their presence by chirping, but stop immediately they became aware of someone approaching. However, their instinct was often to hide on the underside of a leaf, and their outline could easily be seen with a torch beam powerful enough to make the leaf translucent. They could then be swept into a net, or knocked off the leaf by hitting the branch with a pole.

Dennis and Doug walked towards the river and the bridge, playing their flashlights on the foliage as they went. The rain had held off. The plan was not to venture into the deep forest, but to explore the bank of the river and the patchy tree cover at the bottom of the valley.

It was almost as hot as during the day, and the chaotic, insistent chorus of insects was almost overwhelming. Soon they had a dozen specimens packed away, but many more had eluded them by leaping out of the pools of light from their head torches and into the endless darkness.

After a couple of hours they were beginning to flag. Dennis stopped, hands on hips, and gazed at the tropical sky. They switched off their lights and looked at the stars, so much brighter here, away from the light pollution of cities.

'You want to do any more?' he said.

'No, I think I'm finished,' said Doug. 'I bet that little bastard is sitting halfway up a tree somewhere laughing at us.' He took off his backpack and reached into it. There was a clinking sound. 'Tell you what, though. Fancy one of these?'

Dennis flicked on his head torch and saw two bottles of Imperial, the national beer of Costa Rica. 'I think we deserve these,' said Doug. 'Fancy drinking them down by the river? We could pop them in the water for a bit to cool down… What do you think?'

Dennis smiled. 'Definitely,' he said, 'bloody good idea. You lead the way.'

They sat under a near-full moon on a ledge of rock and drank, neither feeling the need to fill the silence.

And it was there, among the mossy boulders of the bank of the Orosi River, that they heard it. A pulsing insect song: unfamiliar, loud, clearly audible above the background rumble of the water, and of such a high pitch that it seemed to drift in and out of the range of their hearing.

They put their beers down and picked their way through the rocks, standing together, straining to locate the source of the sound. Here, out of the canopy of trees, they could see each other's faces in the moonlight. Doug lifted his net and pointed with the handle to an overhanging branch silhouetted against the milky sky.

'I see it,' he said. And then, as he stepped closer, almost close enough to scoop it out of the tree, it launched itself into the night air: a spectacularly large katydid, illuminated in the white beams of their head torches, transforming itself into a flame of living colour as it spread its wings.

And Doug launched himself after it.

§

Westhampton Museum, March 2019

Matt was trying not to work too late. Helen was right to insist he came home at a decent hour. The baby would be here soon, and she was tired in the evenings. There were preparations to be made. And he guessed she was worried. Would this be the pattern for their lives together, she was asking herself, when they were a family?

But the collection had to be put into shape. And he was the only member of staff with the expertise to do it.

It was relatively early, 6.30 pm, by the time he switched off his laptop and began tidying up his equipment. Another tray from the 1987 Costa Rica expedition done: mainly cicadas and a few leafhoppers. He put it back in the cabinet and stood there for a moment, enjoying the silence, the accumulated knowledge around him. A tiny portion of the limitless wealth of species, catalogued and described and categorised. He had to pack up and get home. But first, one more look at *Pterochroza linwoodi*.

He had made no progress in discovering who Linwood was. There was no famous entomologist of that name whom Johnson might have wanted to honour. No superior at the university whom he might have wanted to flatter. Why not name the species after himself?

Matt sighed, moving his head and shoulders to loosen muscles stiff from working at his desk. His inability to answer this crucial question, about the most important specimen in the collection, was getting him down. Time to call it a day.

Back home, when they'd eaten and the dishes were done, they sat on the sofa and Helen listened to him describe the puzzle. She was a business studies tutor, with no life sciences background, but could see why the mystery had lodged in his mind. As usual, she had a direct way of addressing the problem.

'Why don't you ask him? Professor Johnson. He's still alive, isn't he?'

'Yes, but when we got the collection he wouldn't take part in any of the publicity. He's completely retired. Widowed, I think. Never takes part in university stuff, conferences or anything. I couldn't just phone him up out of the blue and ask him a question like that.'

He thought for a moment. 'I need to see him, I think. Apart from anything else, it's mad that I've been working on his collection all this time and I've never met him. But how I'm going to lure him out, I've no idea.'

'Well, what about if you got him to do something low-key, not in the public eye, but really worthwhile, that he would find difficult to refuse. Get him along, get to know him and then have whatever conversation you need to have, face-to-face.'

'Get him to do something? Like what?'

She rolled her eyes. 'Like that family open day you were thinking of having. July, was it? Why wouldn't he come to that?'

Matt thought about it. He had been considering a summer educational event in the museum's spacious grounds, a large proportion of which had been set aside for native wildflowers, providing a flourishing habitat for all kinds of small creatures. The day would include bug-hunting and pond-dipping for smaller kids, and a tour round the collection for older ones and adults. However jaded and reclusive old Johnson was, could he turn down a plea to help young people appreciate the natural world?

'I think you've got an idea there,' he said. 'The university will have his email or his address.' Then a thought struck him. 'But…'

'What?'

'Would you be able to come too? We'll have the baby then. He, she… it'll only be a few months old.'

'Why not? By then we'll be old hands at going out with a baby in tow. You go ahead and organise it, and we'll be there as a family.'

§

The Blue Bell, Westhampton, July 2019

Matt brought two pints to the alcove table and Dennis gripped one with an arthritic but steady hand. He took a sip before setting it down.

'Thank you,' he said. 'Not just for the beer, I mean. Thanks for the day. I thought it went really well.'

'No, thank you,' said Matt. 'It's just so exciting for people, if they're interested in natural history, to have someone around with so much knowledge. You had those kids absolutely entranced.'

Wearing a straw hat and a badge reading The Bug Inspector, Dennis had sat at a trestle table in the grounds, patiently identifying caterpillars, ladybirds and woodlice for a queue of kids. Matt hadn't asked him to put in more than an hour or two, but he'd stayed the whole day, requiring only mugs of tea and a regular supply of carrot cake. As well as inspiring young children and their parents about the living world around them, he'd given invaluable advice to a couple of undergraduate volunteers thinking of specialising in entomology.

And he had charmed Helen. 'Take him for a drink,' she had told Matt as the event had drawn to a close. 'I'm sure he'll take you up on it. He's such a lovely old guy. He doesn't seem like much of a recluse to me.'

Looking across the grounds, Matt had to agree. Everything was packed up, but he could see Dennis still chatting with Terry the caretaker and his son, the boy holding out his palm and Dennis bending over to examine whatever creature the youngster had found.

And now, thought Matt, here he was, in the pub around the corner from the museum, drinking with a quiet, gentle old man in a linen summer blazer, who seemed in no rush to get home.

'Your wife,' Dennis was saying, 'she seems a very capable lady. How are you finding it, being new parents?'

'Well, the baby's going through the night now. But God, I had no idea what it would be like, losing so much sleep. I took a bit of paternity leave but I had to go back to work after a couple of weeks. I'm just getting back into the swing of things now. Luckily, I more or less finished working on the collection before she was born.' He looked up at Dennis with a smile. 'It was a privilege to work on it.'

The old man acknowledged this but made no comment. He took another sip before speaking. 'You know what they say about people in our field, don't you?'

'No, sorry.'

'They say it's always best if an entomologist marries another one. Because we get obsessed. The thrill of tracking something down, something rare or something we haven't seen before, and then the pleasure of classifying it, categorising it. The satisfaction of placing it in a system of knowledge. We devote so much to our work, and it's a lot to ask of a partner.'

'I know what you mean,' said Matt. 'Before the baby was born I was putting in some long hours. Helen didn't like it. She was probably right. I don't know if it was strictly necessary. I think having a baby puts all that into focus. The importance of home life.'

'She was right,' said Dennis. 'I lost my wife 12 years ago, and towards the end we had a better relationship. But looking back, I can see what effect my work had. She was a teacher, and she found it hard to understand. The trips abroad, the research when I got back…'

'But look at what you achieved. Your work was so important.'

'Well, it's kind of you to say that. I suppose that's what we hope for, in science, that we'll make progress in what we know, push the boundaries a little further. But…'

Dennis picked up his pint, went to drink, then put it down again. He looked at Matt. 'I'm an old bugger. Sorry, I've probably gone too far…'

Matt held up a hand and shook his head. 'No,' he said, 'you're right.'

They drank in silence for a while, but it was a comfortable silence. The pub was busy enough for there to be a background buzz of chat and activity, but not noisy enough to spoil conversation. And to Matt's surprise, Professor Dennis Johnson wanted to talk. He told tales of mishaps and successes. Of amazing discoveries made in sodden jungles, at roadside truck-stops and under microscopes. Of wrangles with academic authorities, and rivalry with his contemporaries. And then Matt asked him about the Costa Rica trip in 1987.

Dennis sighed, and got up. 'Let me buy a round first,' he said.

'No, please,' said Matt. 'Let me. You've given us a whole day. Let me get it.'

He bought the round and came back to the table. Dennis took a long draught. 'I don't usually drink beer,' he said, 'but on that trip it seemed the thing to do. They had a very good local lager, I seem to remember.' He paused. 'I don't like talking about Costa Rica. You'll understand why in a minute. But I suppose you should know the story. You're the keeper of the *Pterochroza* now, after all.

'So, that expedition came at a point in my career when I was really hungry. I wanted to make my name. I'd been looking furiously for the bloody thing for days, trying to follow an account by a fellow called Korner – one of those amazing Victorian churchmen who stomped around the world collecting anything they could get their hands on. According to him, it lived up in the cloud forest and was active during the day, and I was insistent that we had to put his evidence to the test and give it our best shot. Which meant trudging up steep trails in ninety percent humidity, which was bad enough, or in a tropical downpour, which was worse. Then hours of searching, which turned up lots of fascinating stuff, but not what we were looking for.'

'We?'

'I was with a young colleague of mine, Douglas. A very brilliant PhD student. He was sceptical of my tactics; I have to say. Eventually, on the last full day of the expedition, we changed tack altogether. He suggested we try a nocturnal search, and instead of climbing up into the forest we stayed in the river valley. Right on the banks actually. We were still keen to find it, but this was a last throw of the dice and we weren't being that rigorous.' He took another draught. 'If I recall, we shared a bottle of beer or two.

'Anyway, we heard an unusual katydid song, and Doug spotted where it was coming from, in a tree. And when it jumped, we could both see what it was. Absolutely unmistakeable. Those incredible colours, the eye spots. Just breath taking, even at night, with head torches. And the size. It was just obvious what it was.

'We could see where it landed, so Doug went after it immediately. An athletic chap – he just took off. But it was night-time, and the river bank was made up of large boulders, quite slippery, and he was excited… '

Dennis stopped. He looked helpless. There was a long pause while he searched his blazer pockets, took out a large handkerchief and blew his nose.

'So, Dougie… Doug. He went after it with his net, and he would have got it, but he slipped. He slipped on a rock and he went down hard, really hard, and hit his head. I couldn't tell quite how badly he was hurt, but I could see his head was bleeding, and he'd clearly done something to his leg because he wasn't able to get up. I told him: "Dougie, I'm going to get help. We're going to get you out of here," and I was about to run back to the research station to find the team medic.

'I wanted to go for help. But Dougie said no. I bent down to him – I could just about hear him – and he said no, I had to get the *Pterochroza*. "It's what we came for," he said. I remember him saying that, and I remember thinking: he's conscious, he's talking, he's going to be OK. He spotted the *Pterochroza*, he almost got it, and now I've got to finish the job.

'So I did. It took no time at all. I knew where it had settled, and it hadn't moved. One sweep of the net and I had it. I got in a box, stashed it in my bag and got back to Dougie. "We got it," I told him, "we got it. And you're going to be OK. I'm going to get help and you'll be OK."

'So I left him there, and got help, and we got him back to the research station, but there was nothing the doctor could do. The head injury had caused bleeding under the skull, putting pressure on his brain. Apparently, if you have that kind of injury, immediately afterwards you can have what they call a lucid interval. But then you can go downhill, very rapidly, and Dougie did. He was dead a few hours later.

'And of course, I blamed myself. I should have got help immediately. I should have ignored him telling me to finish the job, get the *Pterochroza*. Above all, I shouldn't have been so ridiculously focused on the thing in the first place.'

Dennis took off his glasses and rubbed his eyes. 'I shouldn't have been so stupidly single-minded, so obsessed with finding it. The cost was too high.'

He put his glasses back on and blew his nose again. 'I'm sorry,' he said. 'You didn't need to hear all that.'

Matt touched his arm lightly. 'Don't worry,' he said. 'I feel honoured that you wanted to tell me. And I don't think you have anything to blame yourself for. It was a terrible accident, but it wasn't your fault.'

'Thank you,' said Dennis, composed once more. 'It's good of you to say so.'

There was a silence. They both took another drink. Matt hesitated, then said: 'The colleague you lost, Doug. His surname was Linwood?'

Dennis nodded. 'I wanted to name it after him, of course. There was no other possibility. I couldn't name it after myself, not after what happened. I decided that straight away, the day he died.

'It was an awful time. The trip was over, and everyone else went back the next day, but of course because of the accident there had to be investigations, and the authorities notified, and proper procedures followed. I ended up staying for a while until all those things had been done and his body could be flown home to his family.

'I remember one afternoon, I was feeling pretty low, and I had nothing to occupy myself with. I couldn't go out collecting. I couldn't even bring myself to look at the specimens we'd got. So I decided to go into Orosi, the nearest town, and just have a look around.

'Really the only thing to see in the town is the old church of San Jose, built in the mid-1700s – apparently the oldest house of worship still in use in the country. It's a beautiful old, white-washed building, with a low-pitched roof and a bell-tower, set against the green backdrop of the mountains. A very special place.

'So, that's where I ended up. It was cool in there, and so quiet. Rough, plain timbers, a tiled floor, a beautiful, ornate red and gold altar. I could hear a dog barking at first, but then that faded away and I was there alone, in the silence. I walked up the aisle and sat on a pew in front of the altar, feeling numb. I think there was a painting of St Francis, the patron saint of animals.

'You're familiar with JBS Haldane, the great biologist?' Matt nodded. 'Well, for some reason, sitting in that church, that famous quote of his popped into my head. You'll recall what he said, when he was asked what he had discovered about God from studying his creation. He said that because of their overwhelming abundance, one would have to conclude that the Almighty had "an inordinate fondness for beetles".

'Not a very helpful theological insight, I think you'll agree. I sat there for a long time, thinking about Doug. About disagreements we'd had professionally, quite vocal at times, and how I'd admired his talent. I knew he would have matured into one of the finest entomologists of his time, with a mind far more able than mine.

'I sat there and thought about his delight in the natural world. Not just his scientific curiosity – his desire for knowledge – which never flagged. I mean his delight in the living things around him. Not just insects, but everything. I wondered if I had that delight. And I thought about him dying, far from home, on some mad quest for a particularly colourful katydid. Which impulse was he following – the desire for scientific knowledge, or his love of nature? Maybe there's no difference. Or was he determined to find it because of me?

'I felt very foolish, very guilty, and very small. All my knowledge seemed pointless. If I'd been a Catholic and there'd been a priest there, I would have gone into the confessional, even though I don't speak much Spanish. But I just sat there and thought about the beauty I'd seen in my career: all those wonderful animals, those pristine environments. I felt so grateful. And I thought about the cloud forest, which Doug and I had explored, which was richer in life than any place I'd experienced, or even knew about. I was grateful that I'd known him, and that we'd seen that place together. But I felt the loss… the overwhelming sadness that he would never have the life he deserved. He would never see any more of the riches that creation had to offer, from its extraordinary variety.'

Dennis exhaled deeply and sat back in his chair. 'I'm sorry,' he said. 'The regrets of an old man. You should get back to your family.'

It was getting late. They drank up, got up from the table and shook hands. 'Thank you,' said Matt. 'Thanks again for coming today, and for talking to me. It's been a privilege.'

Dennis gave a small nod of acknowledgment. 'I haven't spoken about Costa Rica like that for a long time,' he said. 'You've probably heard that I tend to keep myself to myself these days. But I'm not quite the hermit they make me out to be. If you want me to come to another open day, or go on a field trip, I'd be very happy to. Anything that helps people – especially the youngsters – find that joy in the living world. Maybe I'll be around long enough to see your daughter starting to follow in your footsteps.'

They began to make their way through the pub, but Dennis stopped and turned to Matt. 'Teach her well,' he said, 'spend time with her. You never know. She may not be interested, but if she is, if she feels that delight, then nurture it. Keep it alive.'

Something out there

Joe stopped watching Carol polishing glasses for a moment and turned away from the bar to nod a greeting to Graham coming in: seeing him stumble over the worn stone threshold of the pub and come to a dishevelled halt, peering about like he had never been in the room before. As he did every time.

Usually it was a bunch of them on a Friday night, middle-aged guys from the village, drifting into the plain backroom bar one by one. This particular time, early on in the evening, it was just Joe standing there, two sips into his second one, when Graham made his entrance: wearing a bright green beanie hat, although it wasn't that cold outside. He pulled the hat off and ran his hands through his thick grey hair, slowly, like he was trying to gather his thoughts. Look at him, thought Joe, Stan bleedin' Laurel.

'All right Graham?' he said, motioning to Carol – get another one in. Here we go, he thought.

Graham looked around again, eyes wide in his big innocent face. The bar was empty apart from them.

'Just saw a what-do-you-call-it,' he said. A slight pause, then: 'You know, a puma.'

Carol was listening. Leaning in, taking her time, pouring Graham's pint, then holding it up and pretending to check it for cloudiness. Joe knew what she was thinking. This was one she could tell the girls next door in the lounge bar, her mates, who liked the tasteful carpet and the log fire and the fresh flowers. The comfy chairs, more like a home.

'You what?' said Joe. This was a good one, even for Graham.

'Puma. Behind the Co-op. You know, where they have those big bins and all the cardboard boxes in the cage thing for recycling. Where they go and smoke in their tea breaks. Where that wall is, you know, the one with Leonards' garage on the other side, looks like it's going to fall down any minute…'

'Yes, but what do you mean, you "saw a puma"?' Catching Carol's eye, getting that smile. 'It's dark. You sure it wasn't a fox or something?'

'No, definitely a puma,' said Graham, picking up his beer. 'You know, cougar. Mountain lion. Big bugger 'n' all.' He took a long draught, put the pint back on the bar and exhaled, puffing out boyish cheeks. 'Cheers.'

Carol caught Joe's eye again, shook her head. They went back a bit, the two of them. Just friends, of course, nothing more to it than that. Well, not much. The odd little moment after a big party down here, maybe at Christmas, that no one else knew about. A bit of a rapport, you could say, someone to confide in over a smoke, out the back in the car park, if you had something on your mind.

She knew what Graham was like. 'How many did you have before you came out?' she asked him.

Graham pursed his lips and looked at the ceiling, thinking about that one. 'Just a few,' he said. 'I made Mum's tea, got her settled and we watched something on the box. Coronation Street, I think. Might have opened a can or two. Have a laugh if you want,' – Joe and Carol were already sniggering – 'but I'll tell you something. You know a puma when you see one.'

Joe often wondered what the deal was with him and Graham. Many of the regulars couldn't stomach him and his stories. Joe could tolerate him, even summon up some fondness for the idiot at the end of a boozy night. But were they friends? He had certainly never been to the house with the peeling window frames that Graham shared with his disabled mother. They only met in the pub, on a Friday night. Maybe, with his daftness and his bullshit, Graham was just guaranteed entertainment.

What about that time he reckoned his numbers had come up on the lottery, a £1.5 million rollover, only he'd accidentally swallowed the ticket? The time he'd met a woman in Venezuela on the internet, who had asked him to marry her and move in with her and her twin sister? Or the one about his grandfather making a fortune from inventing those little tubes you get on the end of shoelaces, only to blow it all on a dodgy investment at Lloyd's? Or the sinkhole under his shed?

OK, there was the time he'd seen the prime minister going into the parish church. Joe had to give him that one.

Turned out she was attending the christening of a family friend's child. Pictures in the paper the day after, everyone talking about the security guys outside, how she waved before getting into the big black car...

Carol was wiping the bar down with a Heineken towel. They lifted their glasses out of the way to help her. 'You know it's not "pooma", don't you?' she said.

Graham put his pint back down and wiped his mouth with the back of his hand. 'What?'

'You said "pooma", but that's not how you pronounce it. It's "pew-ma". No one says "pooma".'

'OK,' said Graham. 'Pardon me, madame. I didn't know one had to speak posh in this place.' He looked around the spartan bar, which had somehow escaped successive waves of themed interior design ordered by the brewery. 'Must have gone upmarket.' He caught Joe's eye and grinned. Aren't I the joker? said the look.

Oh God, thought Joe. The guy reckoned he'd seen a puma, in Hampshire, on the way to the pub, on a Friday night. And ten minutes into the conversation they were none the wiser as to the details.

'Pew-ma,' Graham was saying, trying out the pronunciation. 'Pew-ma. Peeuww-mah. Anyway, I saw one. Big black thing. Massive. Most amazing thing you could see in your life. I was on my way down here and I decided to come through the churchyard, don't know why. Carried on down King Street and I'm going round the back of the Co-op, and –'

Clive had come in.

'All right mate?' said Graham. Clive hesitated for a second, then realised he was committed. Too late for an about-turn. 'I do believe young Joseph here is in the chair,' said Graham, stepping away from the bar to let Clive in. Joe nodded a welcome and fished out his wallet.

'Guess what Graham's seen,' he said.

'No bloody clue,' said Clive. 'An alien. In the gents. A herd of water buffalo charging down North Street. What's her name, off the 10 o'clock news: Fiona Bruce. Starkers, on a mobility scooter.'

'A pooma,' said Graham.

'A what?'

'Pew-ma. You know, big cat. Saw it behind the Co-op, where they have the bins and that.'

'Really,' said Clive. He had no patience with Graham when he started on one of his stories. They all took a drink in the ensuing silence.

'Shall we sit down?' said Joe. 'Then Graham can tell us all about it.'

Clive looked reluctant. He glanced behind Carol through to the lounge, but could see no one he knew in there. No chance of escape. They took a corner table.

Graham was scruffy, haphazardly dressed, always managing to wear something odd that made him stand out. The stupid beanie hat, or orange trainers. A baseball-style bomber jacket with yellow leather sleeves.

Clive, who was ex-navy and ran a successful yacht-hire business, was always smoothly turned out in expensive smart-casual wear. He blended perfectly into the background in what was, after all, a rather well-heeled village.

They got on well enough over a pint, but Clive had little time for anything he considered fanciful. Into this category, along with Graham's tales, he placed the other man's imaginative but short-lived attempts at earning a living – the latest of which involved selling seaweed-extract skin products on a franchise basis, entailing a garage full of bottles of foul-smelling liquids.

Graham was looking at his phone. 'Says here there are currently around two hundred wild cats kept privately in the UK,' he said. 'About fifty of those are your big cats. Clouded leopards, you name it. Blimey. And that's just the ones they know about, the ones that are licensed or whatever. Pretty good chance of a few getting loose, I'd say.'

'What about ocelots?' said Clive. 'Any of them running around?'

'What?' said Graham.

'Ocelot. Type of jungle cat,' said Clive, catching Joe's eye. 'Beautiful coat. You know that painter? Dali, the surrealist bloke. He had one as a pet.'

Graham took this as a serious enquiry. He studied his screen and took a gulp of bitter. He had an annoying habit of swilling it around his mouth. 'Nnn… nope,' he said. 'Nothing about them here.'

'So tell us about it then,' said Joe. 'What happened? You survived to tell the tale.'

'I told you. It was behind the Co-op, by the bins. Saw me and it sort of froze, you know, like a cat does when you surprise it. Then it jumped on top of the wall. It looked at me for a second or two, then… off.'

'You weren't scared then. No change of trousers.'

'Didn't have time to be scared, mate. It all happened so quickly and I was riveted to the spot. Not every day you see one of those things, is it? Beautiful, the way it moved. A truly wild creature…'

He shook his head, slowly, a faraway look in his eyes.

'Crisps?' said Clive, apparently unable to bear this solemn moment any longer. 'Scratchings? I haven't had any tea.'

They decided which snacks they wanted, and another round seemed appropriate, so Clive got one in.

Graham was back on his phone. 'They eat rabbits, raccoons, deer…'

Clive came back. 'You know what,' he said, handing Graham his pint, 'I'd bet you my house and my Merc it was an ordinary cat. Like those Beast of Bodmin photos, where you get a trick of the light, funny perspective, and it looks enormous.'

'No way,' said Graham. 'It was a pooma. Pewmah.'

'Bollocks,' Clive said, and looked at his watch. No one spoke.

'How big was it?' said Joe eventually.

When they found themselves together on a Friday night, he and Clive and Graham, and a few others that came and went, he generally played the straight man to Graham's clown, just to keep the laughs coming. He didn't come down the pub to be serious – quite enough scope for that in real life, thanks very much, when you'd got to a certain age and had been kicked around a bit.

He had taken early retirement after a modest career in newspapers. Perhaps he was spending too much of his spare time, too much of his pension, down here. Too much time listening to the likes of Graham. But he'd been in enough newsrooms to learn the value of a good story, even if it didn't pay to look too closely at the facts.

Graham was contemplating the dimensions of the puma. 'Seven or eight foot,' he decided. 'From this table to the dartboard there, easy.'

They looked at the dartboard. Carol came over to get the empties and the crisp packets. 'You still on about that puma? Graham, you should go round there' – she indicated the lounge and its group of female customers with a jerk of her head – 'they're lapping it up. Half of them are terrified, too scared to walk home.'

Graham didn't need telling twice. He picked up his drink and trotted round to the lounge. Clive scowled at Joe. 'Why do you do that?' he said.

'Do what?'

'Encourage him like that. The man will say anything for attention. Total bollocks.'

Joe had no answer. After another uncomfortable silence, he announced he was going for a pee. On the way back he met Carol in the corridor, headed into the car park for a cigarette. 'You having one?' she said. Joe glanced into the back bar, where Clive sat alone. He would be all right there for a bit.

'Go on then,' he said. 'I'll have to scrounge one off you, though.'

He watched her walk out. Like him: divorced, of a certain age, no kids. She was a good-looking woman, carried herself well. Smart too, had her own accountancy firm until the split meant she had to start from scratch on her own again, a bit of bar work helping to fill the gaps. He liked her scepticism, her common sense. He liked her eyes, alert and alive, and the creases around them when she smiled. He liked the way she rested her breasts on the bar.

She passed him a cigarette and lit it for him, and they stood in the car park for a while, saying nothing. They could hear the lounge bar women giggling at Graham's puma story.

Carol was watching him with narrowed eyes, figuring him out. Wanting him to be the first to say something. He wasn't good at that. It was nice just doing this, smoking together side by side, looking across at each other from time to time.

She took a drag, exhaled and looked at him again, more keenly now. 'Hear anything from the *Gazette*?'

'About what?'

'About freelancing. You said you were going to ask them.' She was right. He'd said something about being bored, wanting to get back in the game. He'd put a call in but hadn't followed it up.

'No, they didn't come back. I didn't push it.'

She was quiet for a while. 'You know,' she said, 'you could do a lot better than this. Hanging around this place, I mean. Listening to Graham and his nonsense.' Joe didn't respond and she was quiet again. Deciding whether to say something, he could tell.

'I'm not staying here,' she said. 'I've given myself a goal. Six months from now, I'll have found a proper full-time job and I'll have put a deposit down on a flat. In town, not here, not in the village. I want a new start. I want to be doing something with my life while I'm still young enough.'

'OK,' said Joe. 'Good on you. I mean, that's great. Good to have a target, set yourself a goal like that. Sad to see you go, obviously.'

Carol stubbed her cigarette out, looked down at the ground. Thinking again, thought Joe. Here it comes. Don't know what, but something.

'OK, I'm going to say it,' she said. 'I can't afford a flat on my own, not to start with anyway. I think we should go in together. Put our savings together.'

'And what? You live there?'

'Not by myself, you idiot. We move in together, that's what I meant. Give it a go. You get back into journalism, or whatever, get a second wind. What are you doing with your life otherwise?'

Silence. He looked at Carol, knowing that he had to say yes. That this was another chance. He met her eyes and nodded, acknowledging she was right. He started to say something.

Then she gripped his arm. Not tenderly – there was urgency in her touch. 'Over there,' she whispered. 'I think you've got a story to sell. A big one. See over there?'

Joe looked down the car park to a fence at the bottom, where it bordered a field: the beginning of endless, open countryside, peppered with dark clumps of woodland. 'See what?'

'Eyes,' she said, pointing to a clump of trees. 'I saw them, reflecting the light from the pub. You know, how a cat's eyes shine in the dark. But it was something big. Bloody huge.'

And as they watched, there seemed to be a patch of darkness that was somehow darker, moving in the gloom. Almost an absence of light, not an object. And with it was something that was like a long, black tail. In a silent, liquid movement, the shape seemed to slip over the fence and merge with the night.

'Hey,' said a voice from inside, and they looked round. It was Graham, holding up his phone. 'It wasn't a puma I saw,' he said, coming towards them.

They stared at him.

'Can't have been,' he said. 'It says here, online, you never get black pumas. If it was black, it was a panther. Probably a type of leopard.' He stood by Carol, shaking his head. 'Wow,' he said, 'a panther.' He looked from one to the other, puzzled at their silence. 'What's up? Did I interrupt something?'

'Give us a minute, mate,' said Joe.

And then they were alone again. Two people standing together on the edge of the darkness, trying to discern what was out there. Trying to gauge the dangers.

Her next door

'OK, go on then,' said Greg, holding out his glass to Janet for another slug of sherry. 'Thanks. I was just telling Clare about last time. I still get shivers thinking about it.

'Just think,' – he turned back to Clare – 'we spoke to the chief maidservant of Cleopatra, right here, in this room. Janet went into her trance, and all of a sudden there was a chill in the air, and we could hear this kind of… *disembodied* voice. She was talking to us. It was incredible. She was like: "Greetings, I am Charmion, maidservant to the Queen of Egypt." Then we all introduced ourselves, and Janet asked if she would mind answering a question. Remember what you asked her, Janet?'

He drained his small glass of Bristol Cream, his eyes on Janet, who had stepped away to straighten a chair at the table. She turned back to them, picked up the bottle and gave him another refill.

Her sherry untouched, Clare waited for Janet's response. The others fell silent. Greg, tall and excitable, early thirties, with a loud shirt and neat beard, had been to the last seance here and had clearly been impressed. Norman, plump and quiet, in a tie and V-neck jumper, apparently a regular, seemed weighed down with some secret burden. Clare guessed he was in his early seventies, nearly three times her age. She had Greg down as a spiritual sensation-seeker, a paranormal junkie. But Norman…? She wondered if he, like her, was grieving for a loved one and in need of consolation.

On arriving at Janet's semi-detached home she had been forced to squeeze between a privet hedge and a large new BMW to get to the front door. Greeted by their host, a thin, rather over-dressed woman in her mid-sixties, she was shown through to a recently-fitted kitchen-dining room at the far end of the hall, with expensive Italian floor tiles and huge bi-fold doors that opened to the garden. She was introduced to the two men, given a sherry and shown the nibbles. The three of them were then left to chat for twenty minutes, until Norman said he would go and check if Janet was ready for them. After five minutes he returned to report that yes, they could go through.

Now they were in the small living room, where the pale glow of the streetlights was shut out by thick black curtains across the bay window. The table was covered in dark red velvet cloth, hanging almost to the floor, with an ornate candelabra in the centre. Its candles were alight, and there were others in the fireplace and around the room. The main ceiling light was dimmed. A couple of armchairs had been pushed into corners, and the large television had been covered by another dark cloth. The shelves held a few books on spiritualism, cookery and gardening, and many ornaments – mostly ceramic animals, and souvenirs from Mediterranean holiday destinations. There was only one picture, above the TV. It showed a cottage in a woodland clearing at night, an unnatural glow emanating from its windows. Clare wondered if this was meant to indicate cosy domesticity or an otherworldly presence.

Several large and garish Persian rugs were spread across the floor, reaching under the table, giving a queasy effect next to the bold swirls of the carpet and the splashy floral design on the wall shared with the house next door.

Janet straightened the edge of a rug with the toe of a patent leather shoe and glanced in the big mirror over the mantelpiece. She patted her cropped blonde hair, which showed dark roots, and smoothed down her skirt. She was ready to pick up the story of Charmion's visit.

'Yes, I remember,' she said. 'I asked her: What is an asp, exactly? Is it like an adder? Or a cobra-type thing? Or really big, like a python?'

Greg interrupted. 'It was fascinating. Ancient Egypt is so cool. Before then, to be honest, I wasn't even sure if an asp even was a snake. We were all dying to know the answer, weren't we Janet?'

Janet gave him a look, then turned to Clare. 'I thought it was a good question to start with, not too personal. She explained that an asp's like a small viper, a bit like our adders, and very poisonous.'

'Very interesting, it was,' said Norman, nodding vigorously. Clare was surprised to see him so animated.

Janet continued with the story. 'Then I asked her: When she was there, in Cleopatra's bedchamber, did she have any second thoughts about killing herself, you know, when it was her turn to get bitten?'

Janet paused. 'I could tell it was difficult for her. Her voice was very shaky, very faint, and I thought we might lose her – that I'd gone too far. I could feel her pain in me, too, as I channelled her spirit. It was overwhelming.'

She glanced around the room, as if to make sure everyone understood the gravity of what she was saying. 'We mustn't ever forget that those on the Other Side are just like us. They're people, with feelings. Talking about how you died is bound to be emotional, when you think about it. It's not going to be easy, even if it did happen more than two thousand years ago. Plus, we have to remember, she saw Cleopatra die first, and her friend, the other maidservant. It must have been terrible for her.'

'So what did she say?' said Clare. Perhaps Janet was building dramatic tension.

'She said – don't you like sherry?'

'Sorry?'

'Your sherry, you haven't touched it.'

'Oh, yes,' said Clare. 'No, it's fine, really. I was just so engrossed in the story, and forgot all about it. This is my first one, my first seance, and I'm a bit nervous, you know.' She took a sip. 'Yes, very nice. So… you were saying, about Charmion.'

'Yes,' said Janet. 'I asked her if she'd thought about not going through with it, and she was very clear. She said: "Janet, my only thought was to serve my queen. I let the snake – the asp – bite me and then my concern was only to ensure that her body was properly arrayed, for when it was discovered. I managed to arrange her crown on her head before I became too weak, and collapsed at her side."'

Greg placed a hand on his breast and shook his head slowly. Norman stared at his feet.

Clare took a bigger sip. 'So moving,' she said, trying to strike the right balance between solemnity and awe. 'I wish I'd been there.'

'She may decide to visit us again,' said Janet. 'Of course, I can't control who'll choose to speak to us from the Other Side, but we've been fortunate to have had some wonderful people. Just ask Norman – he's been to lots of our evenings. Who do you remember, Norman?'

Clare watched him slowly bring his hands together, as if in prayer, and touch his upper lip with his forefingers. He looked anxious about being put on the spot, but determined to pay proper tribute to Janet's skills as a medium. 'Let me see,' he said. 'We've had Running Hare – he was one of Geronimo's braves – and Anne Boleyn's lady-in-waiting, Lady, um... Zouche. And Jan, the Polish airman, who was in the Battle of Britain. And we had that other Indian chap – I mean Native American – who helped the settlers get through their first winter…'

'Soaring Eagle,' said Janet.

'Yes,' said Norman, 'Soaring Eagle. And we had the pirate, Blackbeard, and just before Christmas, which was lovely, we had Catherine the Great. Of Russia. We're very lucky to have Janet.'

Janet looked humble. 'As I say,' she said, 'we never know who will come when we reach out. But we have been blessed.'

Clare looked concerned. 'But…' she began.

'Mmm?' said Janet.

'You do contact ordinary people too though, don't you? I mean, you reach out to people that we've lost, in our families? That's why I'm here. I'd really like to hear from my dad. He passed last year and it would mean so much if I could get a message from him, or just know he's OK.'

She put her hand over her mouth and blinked back tears.

'Of course,' said Janet. 'That's what my evenings here are all about. When we reach out to the Other Side we do have visits from fascinating people, like the ones Norman mentioned, if we're lucky. But I know I've also been given these gifts so I can contact ordinary folk who've passed on – loved ones who are important to us. Don't worry about that.'

She smiled thinly and patted Clare's arm, then addressed the room. 'Right, everyone, I think we're ready. Norman, do you want to sit in your usual seat?'

A large chair, its arms and high back draped with heavy black cloth, had pride of place at the table in front of the curtains. Clearly, this was Janet's. Norman sat down to the left of it, next to the door to the hall. Janet motioned Clare to the chair opposite hers, while Greg took the remaining seat to the right, in front of the floral wallpaper.

Before taking her own seat, Janet switched off the ceiling light and put out the candles around the room with an antique-looking bell-shaped snuffer. Then she sat down and began to extinguish the candles on the candelabra until only one was still flickering.

'Let us begin,' she said. 'Now, everyone hold hands. Don't let go, please, or you will break the circle. Just relax, and be open to whoever wishes to meet with us tonight.'

Clare took Greg's hand in her right, and Norman's in her left. Norman's hand was clammy, with a loose grip, while Greg clasped her hand firmly, holding on as if they were about to start a rollercoaster ride. She could feel small quivers of excitement as he prepared for the evening to unfold.

Then Janet put out the last candle, and they were in total darkness.

She was silent for some minutes, then gave out a soft moan. A louder one followed, then a deep sigh. It seemed the air in the room had suddenly cooled. A draught had sprung up around their feet. Clare shivered.

A few more minutes passed, and she could feel Greg beginning to fidget. 'Aaaaaah…' said Janet eventually, exhaling deeply. 'Those on the Other Side are reaching out to us. We must open our minds and our hearts to welcome them.'

Another long moan followed, then: 'I can feel… I'm sensing… there's someone on the Other Side who wants to speak with us. Who desperately wants to speak to us, to *one* of us. They passed over recently, very recently. I see a name, beginning with B…'

Clare squeezed Greg's hand. Her father had been called Bill.

'A name… beginning with B…' said Janet, in a low murmur.

Then there was a noise, like the erratic ticking of an electric kettle beginning to heat up. An odd smell filled the room: a blend of boiled cabbage, Persil washing powder and stale perfume. Greg began to wriggle in his seat.

'A man's name, beginning with B…' said Janet.

'Bollocks,' said a clear female voice. 'Oh, sod it. Hang on a minute.'

A faint luminous patch appeared on the wall to Clare's right, the one shared with the house next door. The voice was coming from this area of luminescence, which was now becoming more intense. An area of floral wallpaper seemed to dissolve, become an opalescent pool of light. It began to swirl, and the voice could be heard again.

'Ooof!' it said. 'Nearly there, don't mind me.' And then they could see the head, shoulders and arm of a middle-aged woman, wearing hair curlers, emerging from the swirl. She grimaced as she strove to extricate the rest of her body.

'Ooof! Bugger, that's my tights laddered. Hang on, this leg's stuck. No, here we go…'

And then, accompanied by a sound like the popping up of a toaster, she gave a final grunt, pulled a foot through the wall and was there before them, in the living room, brushing down her blue nylon coverall and peering around her. The shimmering area of wall became dim, and then faded into the darkness.

'Ooh,' said the woman. 'I'll never get used to that business, going through walls. It's not easy, I can tell you. Let me catch my breath.'

They sat in the darkness for a while, in stunned silence. Then she spoke again.

'Who forgot to pay the leccy bill? It's as black as our bloody coal shed in here. And it's freezing.' She paused, and cackled. 'You could catch your death.'

Clare let go of Greg's hand, jumped up and found the light switch.

'No wonder it's so chilly,' said the woman. 'You've got that bleeding fan going down there, haven't you?'

Clare bent down, lifted the red cloth and looked under the table. A small electric fan was whirring away silently. Its lead ran under one of the rugs, emerging at Norman's chair.

The woman was now standing near Greg, opposite Norman, although Clare could see that her pink fur-trimmed slippers actually hovered a centimetre or two above the carpet. Norman was pale, breathing heavily, his hands writhing in his lap. Janet was still, sitting upright, staring at the new arrival, her face blank with terror.

'Whoah,' said Greg, half panicked, half thrilled. 'What's going on? Janet, what's happening?'

'Don't get your knickers in a twist, everyone,' said the woman, catching Clare's eye and grinning. 'I'm from next door. Thought I'd pop in and see what you're getting up to.'

Janet stirred. 'You…' she said. 'You – you're a spirit. We are seekers. We mean no harm.'

'Cobblers,' said the woman. 'You're seekers all right, but the only thing you're seeking is this.' She rubbed a thumb and forefinger together. She nodded at Greg and Clare, and turned back to Janet. 'How much have you fleeced out of these poor people? And all the hundreds before? Oh yes. I've been watching you. I know your game.'

She turned to Clare: 'Let me see, young lady. Who do you think this fella is?' And with a nicotine-stained finger, she pointed to Norman.

'That's Norman,' said Clare. 'I only met him tonight. He comes to the séances.'

'Séances?' said the woman. 'Séances my arse. He's

married to Lady Muck here, sat in her big chair. Has been for forty years or more. Pretends to be a punter so he can get up to all kinds of funny business behind the scenes. Isn't that right, Norman?'

Norman bent forward in his chair and put his head in his hands, now almost curled into a ball.

'Why do you think he was here first? Because he's been here all day. Because he lives here. And why do you think he got you chatting in the kitchen beforehand?'

Janet muttered something.

'What was that, love?' said the woman.

'Kitchen-diner,' murmured Janet. 'It's a kitchen-diner, for entertaining.'

'Pardon me,' said the woman, and sniffed. 'Anyway, I'll tell you why he got you in there, while his other half was lighting her fancy candles. It's so he could get you chatting about your life, the people you've lost. All your information, so she knew what questions to ask.

'Oh yes, love,' she said to Clare, who had begun to cry. 'That's how she knew you had someone beginning with B. Old Norman's got a microphone hidden in the spice rack, hooked up to this room here.

'See all these rugs? They've got wires underneath them running all over the place. They've got gadgets for making spooky noises, blowing air around, you name it. I haven't worked out where it is yet, but old Janet here has got some kind of gizmo that makes her voice sound different, and sends it through a speaker. They've got all sorts of things hidden away behind cloths. All they have to do, once it's pitch black, is stop holding hands, then they can pull things out of their hidey-holes and work the switches.'

Clare blew her nose and tried to stifle her sobs. 'So – who are you?'

'How long have you got, love? It's a long story. No chance of a brew, Janet, I suppose?' She shot a look at the medium, then rolled her eyes. 'Didn't think so.' She sniffed again. 'Never mind, we can have one later.

'Anyway, I'm Margaret. Used to live next door. When I was young, this house had a young couple living in it. They were big friends with my mum and dad, always having parties in one another's houses. Now, the husband was a bit of a boy. Couldn't keep his hands to himself. And when I was seventeen, he got me alone upstairs, here, and… well, you can guess. I can't say I enjoyed it, but it was exciting – it was our little secret. But then… bun in the oven. Up the duff.

'This was just after the war, mind. I was in such trouble. Not like you lot nowadays, getting away with all sorts. But I never let on who the father was. And of course, he kept his mouth shut.

'My mum and dad got a little plan together with this couple, the people next door. They couldn't have kids, so it was just decided that when I had the baby they would adopt him. I didn't seem to have any say in it. It was awful. They just took him away.'

She stopped and glanced at Norman, who raised his head briefly. He looked stunned, uncomprehending. Janet turned to stare at him, wide-eyed.

Margaret rummaged in the front pocket of her coverall and pulled out a small, grubby handkerchief with M embroidered in yellow in one corner. She dabbed at her eyes. 'You've got me going now,' she said, briefly turning to Clare before addressing her audience again.

'It was hard, knowing your baby boy was being loved and looked after by the people next door. They were good enough people – they said I could see him whenever I wanted. But somehow, having him just next door only made it worse. I could see him, even hold him sometimes, but I couldn't have him. I couldn't stand it.

'But like it or not, I had to live here for another eighteen months until I met someone, got hitched and moved out.

'I married a nice steady bloke, boring as hell, and had two girls. Lovely, they were. They're still alive – one became a GP, the other one went to Australia and married a farmer. I keep an eye on them. But do you know, I was happiest next door, before all that business started. I don't like what they've done to it now, though. All those white walls and plain modern furniture. Like a dentist's waiting room.

'Mind you,' she said, nodding in the direction of Janet's bold floral wallpaper, 'not sure I'd go that far with the decor.'

She turned to Clare, who by now was feeling calmer. 'Now, where was I?'

'You were saying you got married…'

'Oh yes. Quite a nice life. Quiet. I kept the house immaculate, always on my hands and knees scrubbing and polishing. I was a good housewife, always had a decent meal ready when he came home. That was what you did in those days. But bugger me, it was dull. I had a couple of little cleaning jobs, in big houses across town. But I used to live for my Saturday nights down the Coach and Horses with a few of the other wives. We'd get all glammed up and have a few drinks.

'One night, it was 1973, and we were celebrating because Cliff Richard had come third in the Eurovision contest. Nearly won it, too, he did. Anyway, I had one too many, maybe a couple, and on the way home I stepped out in front of a number fifty-two bus. And that was it.

'I can't say it's all that exciting being a ghost, or a spirit or whatever you call it, but at least you get a bit of fun every now and again. You should have seen your faces when I came through the wall…

'And I've always been a bit nosy, so it's nice to go invisible every now and again and see what people get up to behind closed doors.' She indicated Norman and Janet. 'Like the parlour games these two have been playing.'

The room was silent again. Norman sat upright and shifted in his seat, as if he was preparing to make a run for it. Margaret gave him a stare and his body sagged again, head hanging down.

'I didn't finish the bit about my baby,' she said, 'but I'm sure you've all worked it out. Norman here is my boy. He inherited the house and married the lovely Janet here.

'And hasn't he turned out well? Not much of a pension from all those years as a school caretaker, so he dreams up this little money-making scheme, to make sure old Janet can have her holidays in Spain and her new kitchen. Her days doing amateur dramatics came in handy too, I bet.'

Clare saw Norman jerk upright again, his mouth open. He tried to say something but slumped back with a little groan. He looked very unwell. Janet reached out and clutched his arm, shooting a horrified glance at the figure addressing them.

'I could have let them get on with it,' said Margaret.

'I suppose they gave a lot of people a bit of a thrill' – Clare looked at Greg, who shrugged – 'and maybe they gave other people some comfort. But I suppose it was this young lady here who changed my mind…'

Margaret moved over to Clare, the soapy perfume scent trailing behind her.

'It's Clare, isn't it?' she said, and Clare nodded.

Margaret hovered over to Norman. 'I could see how much she missed her dad,' she told him. 'I just couldn't let you two make money out of lying to her. You might be my flesh and blood, but I want nothing more to do with you. The pair of you make me sick – nice and cosy here, dreaming up ways to take advantage of people's grief and sadness...

'I'm going to wait until you've refunded these two here, and then young Clare and I are going to have a cuppa. She can tell me all about her dad. And when I get back, I'll see if I can have a word with him, about getting in touch.'

The man in the car

Kim leaned against the railings, arms folded, watching the nursery school gates close, the other parents starting to disperse. Seeing Michelle there on the other side of the entrance in a knot of people: mainly other mums, a couple of grans, the odd bloke. The group becoming smaller as people peeled off, minds turning to the day ahead. Car doors slamming and buggies rattling emptily away.

Once she got a chance to have a word with her, alone, she would have another go at rousing her interest.

So easy to spot, Michelle. Tall, confident looking. Comfortable with these people, all from the same tight grid of terraced streets near the centre of the city, once housing for thousands of dockyard workers and now increasingly given over to student lets.

Michelle, all skinny jeans and hair up high. Heels, usually boots. They both had two at nursery, and similar daily concerns. Scratching around for part-time work. Trying to hold on to it. Getting the kids to nursery and back, feeding them, clothing them, chasing their scumbag fathers for money.

They were close. But Michelle… she was a little younger, with that easy manner. She was interested in all that stuff they talked about at the nursery gate, all the gossip. And she had the Jack Russell, of course. Always helps if you've got a dog, when you're making conversation.

Kim's flat was on the edge of town, away from the pubs and corner shops of the heart of the city, halfway up a blank-faced block scoured daily by the wind. It overlooked the battered concrete sea wall and the restless, muddy waters of the harbour. The main feature of the landscape, off the main dual carriageway that hugged the shoreline, was a large car park with a fishing pier, some benches and a few rusty telescopes on stands that once, perhaps, offered views of the Solent in return for a coin.

She caught Michelle's eye and waited for her to finish. She knew the other women thought of her as aloof. She lived like them, was a similar kind of age to them, she spoke like them. Like many of them, she was a single parent. She dressed like them too – but she didn't buy cheaply, to cheer herself up on a bad day or to jump on a trend. She had the same budget as them, probably smaller, but bought outfits infrequently and invested in as much quality as she could afford. Some felt she was looking down at them, and were scornful. Others admired her, but from a distance.

Her hair, dyed mid-blonde, was unremarkable, but thick and glossy, usually held in a ponytail, casual strands framing and softening a face which could look stern, even defiant. She held herself upright, carried herself well, with an inner quietness. Her eyes were deep and open, quick to come alive, but wary. You didn't have to get too close to see, around them, the lines left by the past.

Amid the daily melee at the nursery gates, they would often see her standing like this. Waiting, still, with arms folded, eyes narrowed in thought.

A few, like Michelle, were intrigued by her and wanted to get as close as they could. But not many.

Michelle appeared. 'Sorry, couldn't get away. You all right?' She broke off and looked down at the dog, which crouched and shuddered. 'Oh, hang on a sec… '

Kim waited until Michelle had dealt with the mess and had straightened up, swinging the bulging little plastic bag from a newly manicured finger. Then she had another attempt at sparking her curiosity.

'He's still there,' she said, jerking a thumb towards the seafront, 'the bloke in the car park. Saw him on the way here. You know, the one I told you about yesterday? Sat in the car, not moving a muscle. In a bloody great big four-by-four. Why would he be sitting in a big posh car like that for so long? Yesterday afternoon I saw him first, and he's obviously been there all night.'

'Like I said, maybe his missus chucked him out.'

'Maybe,' said Kim. 'But if you can afford a big car like that, wouldn't you go to a hotel?'

Michelle sniffed, rubbed her nose with a forefinger. 'Who knows? If it's bothering you that much, go and ask him.' She shot Kim a puzzled look. 'Why's it so important?'

'I'm just curious. What if he needs help?'

'Some weird bloke who sits in his car all night? Not sure I'd want to get involved, to be honest.'

Awkward silence for a moment, broken by a white van pulling up next to them and a young man in a fluorescent vest getting out, carrying a toolbox. Kim tugged the sides of her jacket across her chest and folded her arms. Tracey hooked her thumbs into her jeans pockets, put her weight on one slim hip and watched him walk past, turning to keep her gaze trained on him. He gave her a smile, but she sniffed and turned back to Kim.

'Look, Sherlock, you do your detective thing, but be safe, OK?' Kim nodded. 'And hey, if he turns out to be nice, or loaded, put a word in for me.'

She made a fist and nudged Kim on the shoulder, smiling. 'Better still, grab him for yourself. Probably more your type anyway, gazing out to sea, thinking deep thoughts. How long has it been, anyway? About time you went on a date, you know. You've got a great figure, a lovely smile when you want to show it. ' Another nudge, a grin. 'Go on, he could be really hot. You don't want me tagging along.'

Kim smiled weakly, watching Michelle hitch her bag on to her shoulder, tugging the dog's lead. Turning to go, heading inland. 'See you later,' she heard Michelle say. 'Got to get my roots done. Let me know if he's the man of your dreams.'

Kim took a deep breath. She wanted to tell her: Listen, I don't dream about men any more. I met too many of the wrong kind, when I was younger, when I needed their money. And you know what, I wish I could tell you about it, but I can't, because you're about the only friend I've got, and can you imagine the conversation? You and me on the vodka and Cokes and I blurt out my big secret? 'So yeah, 'Shelle, before the kids came along I went through a really rough patch and had no money, and I went on the game for a bit. Only for a few months, don't think bad of me. Don't dump me as a mate. Oh, and don't tell anyone…'

'No, it's OK,' she said instead. 'I might go and see if he's still there, but I've got stuff to do anyway. See you later.'

She headed for the seafront car park, into the wind. It was twelve years since she'd last approached a car in that place. She'd finished that way of life that night. But now she had to see if the man in the car was still there. And seeing as Michelle's roots were of such great importance, she would have to do it alone.

§

It was a fifteen-minute walk from the nursery to the seafront, the sky opening up the closer you got, the wind harsher, less predictable. The gulls were louder. Kim could see her block of flats off to the left, the car park straight ahead, the silver Range Rover still where it was the first time she'd spotted it. The dark figure still motionless behind the wheel, silhouetted against the big harbour sky.

She crossed the road and walked into the car park, and for several minutes she just stood there, staring at the man prone in the driver's seat of the Range Rover, trying to subdue the heaves of her breathing, trying to suppress the memories that threatened to overwhelm her.

She remembered car doors opening here, men beckoning her in. She remembered the wind hurling sea spray in her face like a judgement, snatching at the money in her hand. She remembered that night twelve years ago, and the man who didn't open his door, no matter how much she banged helplessly on his window, and the bottle of pills on the seat beside him.

Now, today, another man. Somewhere, she had found the courage to rap on his window, and now there he was, blinking and scratching his head, very much alive. Her legs almost buckled with relief.

He pressed a button and his window slid down. Maybe early fifties. Twenty years older than her. Stubble, shadowed eyes and slept-in clothes: an office shirt and suit trousers. She could see the jacket on the back seat.

'I saw you yesterday, in the car,' she heard herself saying, 'and then you were still there this morning, not moving, and I thought…' She glanced out to sea, almost adrift.

She realised how mad she must sound. He was staring at her, trying to understand what was going on. She pulled her jacket around herself and folded her arms. She saw him drop his gaze, realising she didn't want to be looked at.

'Well, I'm fine,' he said. 'And you – are you OK?'

'Yes. It's just that… it's something that happened a long time ago. Someone died. I mean, they killed themselves in a car. I found them.' He was silent. 'I'm sorry,' she said, turning to go. 'I woke you up. It's fine.'

'No,' she heard him say. 'I mean, you're really kind. Sorry for worrying you.'

She'd taken a few paces when she heard the car door open and realised he was getting out. A wave of fear swept over her, but she glanced round, seeing a short guy, balding, looking like life had given him a beating.

'God, I'm a state,' he said, brushing down his trousers.

His right hand sought his left, fingers gripping a worn wedding ring.

She stopped and turned.

'Look,' he said, 'my wife died a month or so ago. I thought I could keep it together, went back to work, but then – I lost it a bit in the office. They said go home, no problem, get yourself sorted, but I just got in the car and started driving. I couldn't go home. It was the last place I wanted to be, with all the memories. I got on the motorway and I kept driving, just kept going really, until I hit the coast. I don't know this area, I didn't have a plan. I got here and then I didn't know what to do. Just been thinking, I suppose.'

He rubbed the back of his head and looked down at his rumpled clothes. 'Look, thanks again. I'll let you go, don't worry. Sorry if I gave you a fright.'

'It's OK,' said Kim, 'my fault. I'm sorry to intrude. You've had a rough time. Hope you get things sorted out.' And she walked away.

§

By the time she reached the petrol station, about ten minutes up the main coastal road, she felt calm enough to think about what she was doing and to make a decision.

She went inside and bought two cappuccinos and a pack of ready-made sandwiches and walked back to the man in the car. She took a couple of deep breaths, then approached the Range Rover again. He was slumped back in the seat, gazing out to sea.

Another knock on his window, another startled look.

He hesitated briefly, but rolled the window down once more, relaxing once he saw the coffees and the food.

'Got you these,' Kim said.

'Look, you didn't have to. I was just thinking, I need to get myself together and turn round and go home.'

'Have a coffee and something to eat first,' she said. He shrugged, and smiled, and moments later they were sitting on the concrete sea wall, looking out over the water.

He ate the sandwiches hungrily. Together, without speaking, they watched the tide begin to go out, exposing the bed of the shallow harbour. Wading birds began to land, picking their way through the rivulets and channels, stabbing beaks into the mud, occasionally taking fright at an invisible threat and launching into the sky, screaming and wheeling. Out to sea, two giant container ships sat at anchor, motionless against the horizon.

No talking, just watching the tide and the birds and the ships. And then he said: 'So, this man who died. It must have been awful. I guess you were close?'

'No. I, uh, just found him. I was young, it was such a shock, A huge shock – I'd never seen someone dead before. It changed my life. I…'

She broke off, because he had started to cry. She remembered that sometimes the men in the cars would sob, afterwards. This one just cried, quietly, looking at the mud of the harbour, the birds and the sea beyond. And then he began to talk, and she listened, until the wind became cold and it was time for him to get back in his car and go home, and for Kim to pick up her kids.

§

The man in the car

'Nothing happened,' she told Michelle, waiting for the children to come out of nursery.

'Nothing happened. Right. So why are you all hot and bothered? You chat up some bloke who's just minding his own business, in his car…'

'I didn't chat him up.'

'Minding his own business, in a Range Rover, obviously got a bit of money, then you rock up out of the blue and give him some coffee and a sandwich, and next thing you're having a heart to heart. Moving in on him.'

'I didn't move in on him. It wasn't like that. He's way older than me, anyway. Short little bald bloke, well, bald*ing*. I didn't fancy him and I wasn't chatting him up.'

'Well, I bet he fancied you.'

Kim was silent for a while, then: 'It wasn't like that.'

'You got his number, though.'

'No, and he hasn't got mine. I don't even know his name.'

'So what was it all about?'

'I told you. He'd lost his wife, he was in a bit of state, I felt sorry for him. I bought him a coffee and something to eat.'

'Did he pay you back?'

Kim remembered the fiver he tried to make her accept. 'I didn't want to take his money.'

Michelle looked at her. 'Funny way to spend the afternoon, if you ask me. What did you talk about, all that time?'

'I told you. He'd lost his wife. I think, you know, it happens… people open up with a stranger sometimes, they talk about stuff they wouldn't talk about with someone else. We sat there and he told me all about his wife, her being ill and losing her and everything, and it seemed to do him some good, just talking, telling someone about it.

'Then it was time to get the kids. He said thanks to me for listening, and he'd decided to go home. We shook hands and he drove off.'

'So you're together, all this time, but it sounds to me like he did all the talking. Your thing about strangers opening up to each other… what about you? Did you get a chance to tell him about your life?'

'No, not really,' said Kim, with a shrug. The children were coming out of nursery. 'Anyway, there's not much to tell.'

One night of love – eve of D-Day
With thanks and acknowledgement to Barrie Pitt, who was there.

They were so, so young. But to Sheila, squinting out from the stage into the bright lights rigged up in the tent, they looked already old. Every show she did, they looked the same.

She could rarely make out individual faces, peering through the dust-speckled beams of the spotlights, the generators rattling, the smoke an acrid blue haze, and she was glad of that. She could not bear to see faces already old, weary from the fight, though the real fight had not yet begun. Better to see the audience as a uniformed mass, a crowd, not a tent full of young men headed for battle, with young thoughts and young fears.

And out there were the woods. Every show she did, they were there. The woods of southern England, mossy and dappled, criss-crossed with ancient livestock trails worn so deep into the soil that their banks rose taller than a man. Woods of beech and oak and twisted thousand-year-old yews. Old woods, now home to thousands upon thousands of young men, soldiers from a newer country across the ocean, waiting for their orders, to learn what was wanted of them.

They had been here for weeks, waiting and waiting, sometimes idle in hammocks, sometimes tending their vehicles, sometimes breaking their backs smashing rocks, pummelling small country lanes into roads fit for tanks. And the waiting in the woods had made them old.

Sheila's city, with its docks and cinemas and trams, had forgotten this old England with its soft earth and its proud trees. Yet now the woods had been remembered. They had been commandeered, cloven, cleared wherever necessary for buildings and machines. And the sound of the woods was no longer the private skittering of animals but the muttered conversations of young men, waiting, shifting their limbs and stretching as they lounged under a glimpse of English sky.

Heading to a show, bumping along in an anonymous covered truck, her costume and make-up packed beside her, she would listen to the other performers joking, their voices growing quieter as they travelled deeper into the trees.

When they finally bounced to a stop they would have no idea where they were. They were not supposed to know. Somewhere on the south coast of England, somewhere in history.

'Good evening Ma'am. This way Ma'am,' a soldier would say. (She loved that 'Ma'am'.) And she would step down into an early summer evening in the woods, the only woman in a vast temporary encampment of males, and make her way across hard-trodden earth to a huge tent – a makeshift theatre. Here, in a curtained-off corner separated from the rest of the backstage area, with a chair and a mirror, she would ready herself for the concert.

Preparing herself tonight, Sheila had wished she had taken a slug from the flask the musicians had passed around in the truck. The camps had been sealed off for the last couple of weeks, and the tension was now almost unbearable.

Her Jim was already fighting somewhere across the water. And she had promised him he'd have nothing to worry about. She had told him she'd wait for him and wouldn't so much as look at another bloke.

She would not break her promise, and had had no difficulty rebuffing the drunken soldiers who had approached her in pubs, their mouths wet and their speech coarse.

Nor was it hard to resist the clumsy advances of the other performers in her concert party, older men mostly, kept at home because their occupations were vital to the war effort. They were not unpleasant, but once rejected they made her feel she had somehow failed in her duty. Somehow, having spurned them, she now owed them the courtesy of listening to their words of wisdom.

OK love, I know you don't want an old man like me, they would say. But listen, this is wartime, and it's not going to get any nicer, and you should think about having some fun.

She had no desire to heed this advice. She had promised Jim. But some of the young men now gazing up at the stage, old before their time, about to leave the dark woods and cross the cold, grey waves… Her heart lurched when she glimpsed their faces.

Backstage, she had taken a deep breath, dabbed some perfume on her pale neck and listened as Ernest, billed as Enrique the Gypsy Violinist, ended his performance with an off-key crescendo. Only six acts tonight. A bit of lewd comedy from Miss Malarkey the drag queen next, then Tambini the magician with the card tricks, then her to close the show.

She smoothed down the dress her mother had made. She hoped it struck the right balance of girl-next-door wholesomeness and glamour.

She had turned to the mirror and begun to put up her hair when she heard the cough.

'Ma'am?' said a young voice. 'Miss Sheila?'

'Yes, you can come in. What is it?'

'Uh…' The soldier entered, nervously taking in the unfamiliar signs of femininity. He was small, sharp-featured, with sandy hair. His young face was creased and worn.

'Um, I'm to ask if you want a cup of tea, Ma'am. I mean, Miss Sheila. Or anything else… uh, if you wanted anything else before you're on.'

'A cup of tea would be nice. Thank you, Private.'

'Yes Ma'am, be right back Ma'am.'

Another cough signalled his return. She took the tea, sipped it and looked up. He evidently had something to say, so she tried to make it easier. 'Where are you from, Private?'

'Chicago, Ma'am.'

'What do you think of England?'

'Oh, I like it fine Ma'am, only it would be better to see it properly, you know, not in…'

'Wartime, you mean.'

'Ma'am, yes Ma'am. I mean, Miss Sheila.' There was

a silence. Then, emboldened: 'Uh... I saw you sing once before, and you did *I'll be Seeing You*. So, me and the guys, we were wondering... would you be singing it tonight?'

'Yes, I was planning to,' she smiled. 'It always goes down well with you lot.' He grinned, then blushed. He looked up, quieter now, conspiratorial.

'Uh... the guys, they said to me – they know I think you're great – and they said I should ask for a kiss, a peck on the cheek, you know. They said I should... '

'Oh, did they? They think I go around kissing every man who asks, do they? Is that what you think?'

He recoiled at her sharpness. 'No Ma'am, no, I don't. I'm sorry. I'm real sorry.' He turned. 'Please... it was just the guys, and we'd had some drinks, and...'

'It's OK. You go back. I've got to get ready now.'

'OK Ma'am. So long. And I really am sorry.'

And now she was onstage, squinting out through the lights into the haze. She went through her act, working up to *I'll be Seeing You*. Then she waited until the applause finished. 'What's it to be now, for the last song?' she asked them. 'Would you like *Ciribiribin*?' She paused. 'Or *One Night of Love*?'

'One night of love!' they roared, as they always did. She stood, smiling, and waited for the laughter and whistles to abate. And then she signalled to the band, closed her eyes briefly as the opening chords sounded, and began to sing.

After the final notes died away, there was silence. Sometimes the men responded like this, she had learned. Rather than applaud straight away, they paid tribute with a moment of quietness, stirred by the emotion of a song, however cheap and hackneyed.

But this time it was different. They lifted their faces to the top of the vast tent, and then she could hear it too – a harsh, urgent, continuous rumble. She was used to an overhead roar at night, but tonight the aircraft were flying low, very low, headed out across the English Channel, and there was no end to their sound. The waiting was over for these men, and history was about to claim them.

One by one, the young-old faces turned back to her. They watched the tears roll down her cheeks. She spread her arms to take them all in. 'Thank you all,' she said. 'And good luck.'

§

By the time she got back to her dressing room, astonishingly, the small private was there. He motioned to a cup of tea he had placed by the mirror, but avoided her eye.

'What is it?' she asked, more softly now. He fumbled in his pockets. 'Uh... Ma'am, you were just so wonderful tonight, and I'm sorry about before, and I wanted you to have this.'

He pulled out a small wooden cross, roughly carved, and held it out. 'I, um, I whittled it out of a piece of one of those old yew trees,' he said. 'I'd like you to have it.'

She took it from him. He turned to leave.

'Private,' she said.

'Ma'am?'

'Before you go. Come here.'

He stepped towards her, and she took his creased face in her hands and held it. And then she kissed him goodnight.

Mind how you go

The wind was against him.

He was exposed, travelling west on the extreme southern edge of England, sea on one side of the path and the main coastal road on the other, heading for home.

He willed his muscles to move fluidly, stroking the bike's pedals around, maximising the power pushing him forwards, keeping the motion smooth as he fought the brute resistance of the air.

The wind shouldered into him. It was thuggish, unyielding. He tucked in his elbows and ducked down over the handlebars, narrowing his frontal area. To his left, over the mud of the wide, wild harbour, a crescent of gulls scythed into the wind, mocking its onslaught, then turned abruptly and wheeled off to the east, using its rush as a slingshot.

The bike, lighter and more responsive than anything he had ridden when he was younger, had been his retirement present to himself on leaving his job as a reporter. Despite the risks of today's roads, it had reignited a passion for cycling he hadn't felt since his teens.

And he loved the random joys it brought. The moods of the weather, the glimpses of wildlife, the nods of acknowledgement or grimaces of shared pain exchanged with other riders.

Most of all, he enjoyed riding the nine miles of coastal path between his home and the city, where he helped elderly people at a day centre turn their memories into prose and poetry.

Once he'd seen a seal in the harbour. Countless times, he'd stopped to watch some animal amble across his path – a field mouse, a slow worm, a stag beetle. A kestrel would hover above him. Rats would give him a quick, cold appraisal before sliding into the undergrowth.

He saw few people on this route. The odd bird-watcher interested in the waders on the mudflats, perhaps. The occasional fellow rider. One winter morning he'd spent twenty minutes sheltering under a bridge with a German cyclist touring Britain, waiting for a rain storm to pass over. They talked about saddle sores, and Bach.

Retirement from the city's newspaper had come two years ago, just after he turned sixty. He had taken voluntary redundancy and a hefty payoff, much to the relief of his editor, a bland administrator who feared the obsessive way Mike pursued a story, and whose attempts to rein him in had led to explosive scenes in the newsroom.

Mike's wife Sara had given up work as an English teacher around the same time, and their plan had been to do up the house in the winter and spend the rest of the year on walking and cycling tours.

Their marriage, twelve years ago, the second time round for them both, had saved him. Sara had calmed him, focused him on the here and now, not the next story coming along. She encouraged him to moderate his drinking and get fit, spending more time in the fresh air and less in pubs with fellow hacks and contacts. She had shown him this path along the shoreline and taught him to watch and listen to the natural world.

On a bike, as in life generally, she was more observant and less impulsive than him. She would ride behind him, but often spotted hazards ahead before he did, shouting warnings about a dangerous pot-hole or a carelessly-opened car door.

Yet her watchfulness had counted for nothing that early evening a year ago, the October sun hanging low, the starlings beginning their frenzied whirling against the sky, when a momentarily dazzled driver, travelling just slightly too fast, failed to see her on a junction and slammed 1.4 tonnes of dumb metal into her beautiful, fragile body.

It took a while for her to die, but not that long. She was gone by the time Mike could reach the hospital.

§

Wind-battered and weary, he wheeled his bike into the garage, locked it to a heavy steel ladder and peeled off his cycling kit. After a shower he thought briefly about cooking, then opened a beer and switched on his laptop.

A couple of months after Sara's death, when the fog of grief and alcohol and anger had begun to clear, he'd concluded he could probably carry on living – if he clung to the things he knew. He kept cycling, because the interlocking rhythms of pedals, wheels, lungs and heart reminded him he was alive. He could not see much point in working on the house. He left Sara's cookery books undisturbed. But he filled the days well enough.

As well as volunteering at the day centre he started a blog, reporting and commenting on local news. It built up a small following of readers who had an appetite for in-depth reporting not satisfied by the meagre offerings of his former newspaper, which had been shrunken and eviscerated by a succession of profit-hungry owners. He wrote fitfully at first, between relapses into misery and lonely boozing, but then worked out a routine he could maintain, and was rewarded by more and more followers. He was thrilled with the two-way nature of the medium – the way his readers, with their comments and suggestions, developed the stories and pushed him in new directions.

But he was without Sara's caution, without her voice warning him to watch the road ahead.

He had begun revisiting some of the crime stories he had covered in his newspaper days – where miscarriages of justice had been alleged or perpetrators never identified. Back then he had been caught up in the relentless daily churn of news, but now he could look back with a new perspective and ask new questions. It meant many hours in the library trawling through copies of the paper on microfilm, and many more tracking down and then interviewing witnesses, lawyers and retired police.

Now, standing in his small study, one hand holding his beer and the other jabbing at the keyboard, he saw a message on the screen from a name he didn't recognise.

'Were u on the *Daily News* in the early 80s?', Oldtimer59 had posted while he was out. 'Remember the Harrison case? If so, got something for you. Msg me back.'

He put down the beer and sat down to type a reply: 'I remember. Do you want to meet?'

§

Two weeks later he was in the Prince of Wales, near the city's docks, drinking an expertly-pulled Guinness two hours before opening time, and waiting for a confession.

He sipped his pint at a sticky table while Oldtimer59, alias Barry Fitzgerald, the landlord, stood smoking at the bar, waiting for an elderly cleaner to finish pushing a filthy mop around the floor. 'OK love,' Fitzgerald said eventually, 'that's enough. You can piss off now.'

She shot him a puzzled look, but he nodded to the door. 'That's right, I'll do the rest. Now scarper.' He opened the door and watched her go. Then he locked it.

In the old days the Prince had been a good pub for picking up stories, if you could handle your drink and remember what you'd heard the next day. Fitzgerald, a big man, was well-known for his intolerance of troublemakers. Back then, when smoking was still allowed and the city's boozers were even rougher than they were now, the Prince had been known for its particularly colourful clientele. But Fitzgerald enforced a makeshift code of behaviour, and loudmouths, drunks and idiots looking for a fight were promptly and efficiently dealt with. Wearing an expression of weary menace, Fitzgerald would stub out his cigarette, stride out from behind the bar and wade into the blue haze of the crowded pub, hauling the offender off his feet and tossing him into the car park, usually with the aid of his boot.

He was not a big man now. He was crumpled, hollowed out. He shuffled across the room and sat opposite Mike.

'Right', he said. 'Where were we?' But before Mike could respond, Fitzgerald held up a hand. He coughed, horribly, for several moments. 'Started in my lungs,' he said, 'but it's all over the shop now. They reckon I've got a few months, tops.'

'Sorry to hear that, Barry.'

'Yeah. Well, like I said, there's something I want to get off my chest. So to speak.' He laughed, then coughed some more.

Mike waited again. 'So what is it then?'

'Maureen Harrison. Why the Bartons never got charged when she was killed.'

'It was obvious why,' said Mike. 'Everybody knew. Because Barton and his son – Vince, was it? – were in here all night. They had an alibi.'

'And what do you think? Do you reckon they really were in here?'

'Well, that's what you told the cops, if I remember. You saying they weren't?'

Mike took another sip of Guinness while Fitzgerald endured another awful spasm of coughing. ''Course they bloody weren't,' he said at last. 'I had no choice. They came round here the night after she died. Took me round the back there,' – he indicated the car park with a movement of his head – 'and gave me a proper kicking. They told me it was a taster. They'd come back and finish the job if I didn't help them out and say they were in here.'

The murder had been a huge story for *The Daily News*. Maureen Harrison, a painter married to a hospital consultant, had been blasted in the face with a shotgun during a break-in at their home. While the couple slept, two burglars had entered through an upstairs bathroom window, avoiding triggering the alarm, which covered only the ground floor. Downstairs, they disabled the alarm and had almost finished filling their bags with antiques, artworks and silverware when Mrs Harrison came down to get a drink and disturbed them. Her husband arrived moments later to see his wife's body sprawled on the living room floor and two figures disappearing into the darkness down the long gravel drive.

'So what really happened?' Mike asked.

'It was an accident. Vince was only a kid, hadn't been on a job that big before and couldn't handle the pressure. But he couldn't tell his dad he wanted out. So he didn't just have a few drinks to steady his nerves – he popped a few pills as well. High as a kite, jumpy as hell. They'd taken the shotgun in case they needed to scare someone, keep them quiet. But Vince grabbed it and panicked, and shot her. His old man got him home and gave him such a beating. But he was his son…

'They liked it in here because I kept a tight ship – didn't give the police much cause to come round. Nice and discreet. So, I told the cops this is where they were. They're evil bastards, those Bartons. I was terrified, and I had my family to think about, you know? I've never regretted it. I'd do the same again, no problem. But it's different now. My missus died last year, my son lives in Australia, I'm on the way out. That woman never got justice. And you've got this blog thing. Up to you, but if you wanted to, you could get it out. The truth.'

Fitzgerald's fag was finished. He got out another one and lit it. He took a long drag and studied Mike through eyes narrowed against the smoke.

'There's one thing, though. I wasn't brave back then, and I'm not going to be brave now. You can be a hero if you want, but you've got to promise me you won't write anything until I'm six foot under. OK?'

Mike drained his pint. Was he feeling a familiar rush of excitement at the prospect of a great story? Or was it the morning beer on an empty stomach? He held up his glass. 'OK, it's a deal,' he said. 'If you can stretch to another one of these.'

While Fitzgerald pulled another Guinness, Mike fumbled with his phone until he found the audio record function. They went through every detail of the landlord's story. Then they shook hands and Mike got his bike from around the back. Fitzgerald leant in the doorway and watched him put his helmet and gloves on.

'You ride that everywhere?'

'Most places. Locally, anyway. Keeps the beer belly under control.'

'You wouldn't catch me on a bleedin' bike. Not the way they drive round here. Doesn't it worry you?'

'Yeah, it does, but the medics say that for every hour cycling, you put an hour on your life.'

'Bit late for me, mate.'

'Well…' Mike had no answer to that. 'You take care

now,' he said. 'Thanks for the chat. See you later.' He looked back to see Fitzgerald on the doorstep, taking a final pull on his cigarette before grinding it into the pavement.

Three weeks later, Mike went to his funeral. A few of the old Prince regulars turned up, but it was not a big occasion. Then he went home and started writing.

He didn't have a drink until he'd finished and the post was online.

Who killed Maureen Harrison? Was the main title. *Part one: The Prince, the murder and the alibi* was underneath. A teaser piece, re-telling the decades-old story of the crime up to the abortive police inquiry, and hinting at revelations to come. Within hours, the screen had filled up with comments.

§

Two days later, at the day centre, Mike was deep in conversation with a group of elderly women who had worked together in a crisps factory until it had closed twenty years ago. He was trying, amid laughter and gossip about the old times and some near-the-knuckle flirting, to get them to concentrate on the task at hand.

There was a bustle of activity at the entrance and he saw a young woman in a pale blue care worker's uniform struggling to push a slight elderly man in a wheelchair. Mike took in her cleavage, slim legs and glossy long hair. Then he glanced at the two women staffing the reception desk. He saw them take in her rings, high heels and long scarlet nails – and exchange a look. This young woman was no care worker. Or she was a decidedly unusual one.

The old man in the wheelchair began talking to the two staff and pointing in Mike's direction, as if he knew him.

Mike did know him. He caught the eye of one of the staff and nodded: It's OK.

The young woman ignored the frosty glances from the desk and manoeuvred the man's chair, amid much tutting and shifting of furniture, until he was at an empty table next to Mike's. The old man wore a navy suit with a subtle pinstripe and a plump yellow tie. His legs were thin under a plaid woollen blanket.

'I'll get you a cup of tea,' the girl said, and turned to go, but the old man shot out a mottled, thick-veined hand, showing an inch of crisp white shirt cuff and a heavy gold cuff link. Fleshless fingers gripped her wrist and a grimace of pain and fear twisted her flawless features. 'Wait,' he said. His voice was quiet, but it was a voice that did not need to be raised to be obeyed.

'My friend here,' he said, waving a knobbly forefinger in Mike's direction, 'would like a cup of tea too.' He turned to Mike. 'Milk, no sugar?' Mike nodded. 'OK,' said the old man, releasing the young woman, 'two teas. Off you go.'

Mike extricated himself from the group of elderly ladies and instructed them to begin putting pen to paper. He had barely got up when their cackling started up again.

He sat down at the old man's table. 'Mr Barton,' he said. 'Been a long time. That trial – the off-licence robbery, twenty years ago, was it?'

'More,' said the old man. 'But I remember you on the press bench, scribbling away.'

'Every day for what, three weeks, we sat opposite each other? But I don't think we ever spoke. Not a peep. Not even a quote when you got off.'

'No, I don't like reporters. Never have.'

Mike shrugged. 'You still drink in the Prince?'

'Not these days,' said the old man. 'Some of us are feeling our age.'

His shoes, Mike saw, were soft and grey, with Velcro straps, and told a story that the suit tried to hide. He was extremely frail. His gaze was watery, his lips thin and pale.

'So you're not on the *News* now,' said the old man. 'Moved with the times, I hear. Making a name for yourself on the internet.'

'Keeping busy,' said Mike. There was a silence. 'So how'd you know I work here?'

'Like I said. You're on the internet.'

The day centre website – it had a page on his project. 'So what can I do for you?' said Mike. 'Don't tell me.' He held up a forefinger for a while, then smiled and folded his arms. 'You want to do an interview about your long and eventful career.'

Barton stared at him. 'Very funny. But I will tell you something, son. I'll give you some advice.'

'Advice?'

'Good advice, about not raking up the past. Getting rid of that crap you wrote the other day – deleting it – and finding something else to write about.'

The young woman reappeared with two teas and some biscuits on a tray. She put it on the table.

'This is my grand-daughter,' said Barton. She nodded and smiled. 'She's a – she's err…'

'A holistic beauty and wellbeing therapist,' said the woman.

'Yes,' said Barton. 'She's doing OK. Lots of customers. Doesn't know anything about the old days, doesn't want to.' He fixed Mike with his moist eyes. 'Nobody does.'

Mike met his gaze. The old man took a sip of tea, then said: 'They tell me you ride a pushbike everywhere.'

'That's right.'

'You wear a helmet, all that stuff?'

'Yes.'

'Still, bloody dangerous cycling round here.'

'Yes, sometimes,' said Mike.

A silence. The old man sucked down his tea and scowled. 'Lukewarm,' he said. He got out a handkerchief and dabbed his mouth, then motioned to his grand-daughter that it was time to leave. 'You want to mind how you go,' he said. 'There are some nutters out there.'

'I will,' said Mike. He picked up the plate of biscuits. 'Sure you don't want a custard cream?'

Barton twisted round in his chair, and in the watery eyes Mike saw a remnant of fire. 'I wouldn't take the piss, son,' the old man said quietly. 'Just think about that advice.' He signalled to his grand-daughter and she briskly wheeled him out. The hubbub of the room closed over the space they had vacated.

Mike rode home quickly, hurling himself against the wind. That evening, it took him a few hours to write the next blog post. *Part two: The landlord's tale* was a transcript of his interview with Barry Fitzgerald.

All he had to do now was click 'upload' and the story would be out there.

He sat at his desk for a long time. The energy that had propelled him home and kept him pounding the keyboard had drained away. The room had become dim and he could barely make out the photo of Sara on the desk. He poured a slug of Scotch from the bottle at his elbow and wondered: How many extra hours had he put on his life, pushing those pedals round?

And now, did he want them?

He clicked 'upload'.

Then he switched off the laptop and poured himself a large one.

§

The next day he got back on his bike and rode to the day centre as usual. This time the old women were more co-operative and they made some progress. He was tired by the time he finished in the afternoon, and not relishing the ride back.

Outside the centre, he checked his phone. His blog had prompted another flood of responses, along with calls from the *News* and the local radio station.

He got on his bike and looked around the suburban street. Kids were coming home from school. A van was delivering a parcel. He had not been taken out by a sniper hired by the Bartons. His bicycle had not been booby-trapped. It was an ordinary day on the edge of the city.

He put on his helmet and gloves and set off. The traffic was starting to build, and his senses were quickened by the need to stay alert on the road. By the time he reached the coastal path, with the sea air in his lungs and his muscles settled into their familiar roles, he felt energised.

A couple of miles on, he noticed a man with his elbows on the fence that ran along the path, looking out over the mudflats and the sea beyond. A cheap mountain bike was leaning against the fence beside him, with a flat back tyre.

All regular cyclists knew the code. If you saw someone in difficulty, especially somewhere out of the way like here, then you stopped, or at least slowed down, and asked if they needed a hand.

Mike squeezed his brakes and slowed to walking pace. As he approached the man stood up, stepped on to the path and raised a hand.

'You all right there, mate?' Mike asked.

'Puncture,' said the other man, pointing to his back tyre. 'It just went flat all of a sudden. I'm a bit stuck, to be honest. I didn't think anyone would come past.' He was wearing jeans, trainers and a heavy jacket over a checked shirt. He did not look like a regular rider. 'I was going to give it five more minutes and then start walking. You haven't got a repair kit or anything, have you?'

'Yeah,' said Mike, 'we can try fixing it if you want, but it might take a bit of time. Where're you headed?'

'Just going into town. Look mate, up to you, but anything you can do you would be good. I'm fine under a car bonnet, know what I mean? But I'm clueless with these things.' He gave his bike a light kick.

Mike propped his own machine against the fence. Turning the other one upside down, he began inspecting the tyre, which was completely deflated, for a sharp object.

'Been watching those, over there,' said the other man, looking over the mudflats and shallow channels of the harbour, where several shore birds were feeding: poking long, curved bills into the silt.

Mike looked up from his task. 'The curlews, you mean? Yeah, I'm always amazed what you see along here, with the main road so close.'

'You into birds?' The guy seemed excited to meet a fellow enthusiast. Mike waggled his hand to indicate a passing knowledge. 'Well, I'm impressed,' said his new acquaintance. 'None of my mates would know a curlew if it came up and pecked them on the arse. They reckon I'm one of those twitchers. But I just like being still somewhere and seeing what turns up, you know? I had no idea this was such a good spot.'

'You don't live round this way, then.' Mike said. The guy was shorter than him, also younger. Powerfully built, with quick, keen eyes that flicked up and down the cycle path before returning to the shoreline.

'No, I'm down from London for a job. I work down here quite a bit, mind you' He gestured up the scrubby embankment to the road. 'But I'm ususally driving. You certainly see more on a bike.'

'Especially if you get a puncture,' said Mike, bending down to the tyre again. The man grunted, acknowledging the joke. He lit a cigarette.

'Want one?'

'No thanks,' Mike said, rotating the wheel slowly as he examined it. 'So what kind of stuff do you do?'

'Bit of security,' said the man. 'Nightclubs and that. Some other bits and bobs – it depends.' He scanned the path again. 'All a bit under the radar, as far as the tax man goes.' His gaze returned to the harbour. 'Shit,' he said.

'What's up?'

'My binoculars. Didn't think to bring them. I think those are godwits over there, but I can't see 'em properly.' He stroked a stubbly chin. 'I bet you get Brent geese here too, don't you?'

Mike knew the small, chattering geese that flew in every winter. 'They'll be here soon,' he said, 'my wife used to look forward to seeing them every year. She was the real bird-watcher.'

'So you're on your own now, then?'

The directness of the question surprised Mike, but he decided he didn't mind.

'Yeah, she died a year or so back.'

'Sorry mate,' said the man. 'I didn't mean to…'

'No, you're all right.' Mike had found nothing in the tyre, nor any obvious damage. He straightened up.

'I can't get my missus out anywhere like this,' the man was saying. 'Not a chance. Shopping's about the only thing she's interested in. Know what I mean?' He took a look up and down the path. Those quick eyes again. Then he turned back to the harbour. 'Did you know, Brent geese are actually smaller than some ducks?'

'No,' said Mike, 'is that right?'

'Yeah, but they're really powerful fliers. They breed further north than any other goose – right up in Siberia.' He took a last drag from his cigarette and stubbed it out on the fence. Another glance along the path. 'Amazing, they are.'

'Yeah,' said Mike. The guy certainly knew his birds. 'Well,' he said, 'I can't find anything stuck in your tyre.

Want me to try mending the puncture?'

'Would that be OK, mate? I feel like I've taken up too much of your time already.'

Mike shrugged. 'No problem. Happy to give it a go.'

He went to his own bike, opened a pannier and took out his pump and repair kit. He was starting to feel cold. The screams of gulls pierced the dull roar of the traffic just metres away, up the embankment. The rush hour was in full flow.

'I reckon they are godwits,' said his companion, looking out over the mudflats again. 'But I can't see if they're the bar-tailed or the black-tailed ones. What do you think?'

Mike turned to look at the group of long-legged birds at the water's edge. 'Sorry, you've got me there,' he said. Sara would have known.

He bent down again, removed the wheel and checked the inside of the tyre for a protruding thorn or flint. Nothing. He checked the inner tube for a leak, again failing to find anything that could have deflated the tyre so dramatically.

'Weird,' he said to himself. He refitted the tube and put the wheel back on the bike. A few strokes of the pump told him what he suspected – the tyre was inflating normally.

Suddenly his companion was bending at his side, prodding the rubber tread with his thumb. 'Wow,' he said, 'nice work. No idea what you did, but do you think that'll get me home?'

Mike nodded. He felt uneasy at the man's proximity. He finished pumping up the tyre and they both stood up.

He stepped back a few paces to his own bike and turned to pack his stuff away. He knew that a tyre that had gone flat so suddenly and completely did not happily pump up hard again and stay that way. There was something wrong. He tried to think it through. But now the other guy was back beside him, advancing with a grin and an outstretched hand.

'Look, thanks mate – really appreciate it,' he said, taking Mike's hand, and they shook.

And as they did so, the keen eyes flashed up and down the path once more. And the handshake became a savage tug, jolting Mike off balance, into the embrace of the younger man, who in the same instant pulled his left hand out of his jacket pocket and thrust a knife deep, deep into Mike's side.

Mike pitched backwards on to his bike. There were two more thrusts. They felt like hard punches. He dropped to the cold ground.

A final flash of the eyes, up and down the deserted path. Then the man scrambled up the bank to the roadside. A car door slammed and an engine snarled into life. A few gulls shrieked into the wind. The noise of the car was lost in the traffic's rumble.

§

Mike remembered being with Sara near this spot, one autumn afternoon like this. A flock of geese had alighted softly on the water, welcomed after 4,000 miles by just the two of them, and a pale English sun hovering low over the harbour.

Then the sky closed in on him and the wind took his thoughts.

The kindness of strangers

'Ah,' said Uncle Francis, 'I see you've noticed the cabinet of curiosities.'

Seated heavily in his worn armchair, he pointed a thick, ponderous thumb over his shoulder, indicating the glass-fronted display case behind him. Facing him, I could see enough of the objects it held to appreciate what an odd collection they formed. A corn dolly, several mother-of-pearl buttons, a faded sprig of heather, a lustrous piece of dark wood carved into the shape of a crouching hare, worn smooth by handling…

'You know the story?' he added. I shook my head. Nor did I want to. After our weighty evening meal and several glasses of Malbec, he had lapsed into a surly drowsiness. He had said barely a word at the table, preferring to motion impatiently with a leathery hand if he wanted the salt or the water jug, rather than bothering to ask out loud.

This suited me. I was only here for one night and I had no interest in getting to know him. I hoped to continue to avoid conversation for the rest of the evening and watch TV instead. My job interview was tomorrow morning and it would have been good to relax. But no, the old sod had seen me glance at the cabinet, and now he had perked up all of a sudden. He would no doubt take delight in subjecting me to some rambling and entirely unreliable tale, dredged from whatever was left of his memory.

It was something my mother had warned me about – once she'd set it all up for me to visit him.

'If your interview's near Oxford then why not stay with my Uncle Francis?' she had suggested. 'You'd save on a hotel and you haven't seen him since you were little.'

'But I don't know him,' I'd protested. 'Isn't he the one that used to be an English professor at one of the colleges but got kicked out? The miserable one?'

'Eccentric,' she countered. 'I think there was some kind of clash of views. Maybe he's mellowed. Anyway, you can talk about literature. He's an author.'

'Mum, are you joking? I've just got a 2.2 in creative writing from a university that's only twenty years old and I'm going for a job in marketing. He's going to love giving me a hard time. On my course we hardly looked at anything written before the 60s, for God's sake.'

On the other hand, I would save on a hotel. I had no money and hated asking my parents for cash. Until I landed a decent job I would be skint. But if this interview worked out, I'd be rolling in it pretty soon. My interview was for a post with a major charity, and if you were good they paid extremely well, especially if you knew your way around digital – no matter what you were flogging the punters. Sick donkeys, sad old ladies, starving brown kids, whatever.

In the meantime, every little helped. So Mum had called Uncle Francis and made the arrangements. She hardly knew him – he was the brother of her father, the elder by more than ten years – but she'd always been a great believer in family.

Dear old Uncle Francis, it transpired, was not of the same view. Although he had been cajoled into accepting me as an overnight guest – Mum is not one to back down from a challenge – it did not follow that he would accept the situation with good grace.

He lived in a commuter village not far from Oxford. I had hoped for a lift from the station, but these days, apparently, Uncle Francis didn't like driving, and petrol was expensive. So I had to get a taxi.

Dodging a fat woman with a pushchair and too many children, then overtaking a smug business type preoccupied with his phone, I emerged from the station well ahead of my fellow passengers and with a good chance of claiming the first cab. Conscious I was wearing my new interview suit and shoes, I stepped carefully around the usual detritus associated with public transport in the UK: a takeaway milkshake carton in a sticky pink puddle, a box of partially-gnawed fried chicken, a dull-eyed homeless guy slumped against a wall, holding out a grimy palm.

He had the same luck with me as did the taxi driver. A scruffy, over-talkative woman, she delivered me to my destination, asked for £8.50, then attempted to get away with the old trick of holding on to my £10 note, as if I wasn't expecting change – assuming I would end the embarrassing stand-off by allowing her to keep it. Nice try.

It was a large house surrounded by a high wall, far past its prime. I walked up a gravel drive that had lost its battle against encroaching weeds and rang Uncle Francis's bell. For good measure, I gave the knocker what seemed to be the first good workout it had had for a while. I was still left studying the peeling front door for some time before the old boy showed up in slippers and stained trousers and we shared a perfunctory handshake. 'So,' he said, 'you're Karen's lad.'

'Yes. It's Charles. Thanks very much for this. I didn't want to put you out…'

'I struggle to keep up with all your names,' he said. 'Breed like rabbits, your side of the family.' I stood in the hallway with my overnight bag and gazed at the woodchip wallpaper.

'Hmmph,' said Uncle Francis, breaking the silence, and I followed as he shuffled off into the interior. 'You can have the room at the top of the stairs there,' he said. 'First on the right.' There was a pause, as if he was struggling to remember the expected social niceties. 'Have you eaten?'

'No, sorry,' I said. I'd assumed that food of some kind would be provided, but it seemed this aspect had not occurred to Uncle Francis until now. Or maybe he had hoped to avoid it.

'I see,' he said. 'I'm not sure we anticipated you needing a meal. Well, I'm sure Mrs Waldegrave can sort something out. The housekeeper,' he said. 'Comes in most days. Not a bad cook if you don't mind it either raw or burnt. I'll tell her it'll be two of us.'

Standing awkwardly at the bottom of the stairs, hands in his pockets, he glanced into the living room, where I saw he had a book open on an armchair. Clearly, I was keeping him from his reading.

'First on the right,' he repeated, and nodded up the wide, thinly-carpeted stairs, before heading chairwards.

I hung up my interview suit in a musty wardrobe. Then, using a small basin by the window, I washed my hands and face. I sat down on the bed for a while, reluctant to go downstairs. Then I opened the door to confirm what I thought I'd seen on the landing. Yes, it was a broadband router, and the access code was taped to the back. I took out my phone and tapped it in. Now, back in my room and with free internet access, I made myself comfortable. It was a good time to satisfy my curiosity about Uncle Francis's departure from the university…

Eventually there was a knock and a woman in a blue nylon apron announced she was the housekeeper, she was pleased to meet me, it was very nice to finally meet another member of the family, and dinner would be in ten minutes.

I closed the door behind her and wondered how she felt about working in the home of a man who had been severely censured by a disciplinary panel for inappropriate conduct regarding a nineteen-year-old female student. He had been banned from contact with undergraduates, and had quietly taken early retirement a few months afterwards, when the dust had settled down. She had declined to press charges, so he had escaped a criminal investigation. But many more students had gone public after the case, claiming they too had been victims of his straying hands. Clearly, the most recent occurrence had been the final straw for the academic authorities.

Maybe, I thought, being middle-aged and decidedly unattractive, Mrs Waldegrave felt relatively safe.

And now, after liver and bacon, here I was in the dusty living room of Uncle Francis's huge decaying house, faded velvet curtains across the rotting sash windows, heavy red wine in heavy cut-crystal glasses, the old TV stubbornly off, trying to maintain a look of polite anticipation as he prepared to launch into his story.

He shifted his bulk and rubbed the rims of his cavernous nostrils with the knuckle of a thick forefinger – yellowed, presumably, from a lifetime of smoking. Thankfully, I could see no evidence that he still had the habit. Maybe he had given up for the sake of his health. It had certainly not improved his temperament.

I waited while he drained his glass with a noisy gulp and immediately refilled it from the bottle on the small table by his chair. My glass had long been empty, and seemed destined to remain so. I reckoned he was getting through the Malbec at a rate of three glasses to my one.

'All those things in the cabinet belonged to my Aunt Jessica,' he said. 'No idea what relation she would be to you. She died before I was born. But this was her house. My parents took it on somewhere down the line and then, well, here I am now. I manage to look after the old place somehow. Constant battle.'

We were interrupted by Mrs Waldegrave, who meekly knocked the door and took half a step into the room. 'I'll be going now then,' she said. 'The dinner things are all washed up and…

'Yes, yes,' said Uncle Francis. 'You'll be in tomorrow? The spare bed will need stripping.' He glanced sourly at me. I was guilty not only of domestic disruption, but of plotting to inflict unspecified indignities on the bed linen.

'Well,' said the housekeeper plaintively, contorting her pudgy features. 'I usually do the bedclothes on a Thursday…'

'No,' the old man said. 'I'd prefer it if everything was shipshape and back to normal tomorrow.' For the first time, he cast a look at her. 'If that's all right with you,' he added, in a tone that implied that it would be.

She left the room and I heard the front door close.

'Dreadful old bat,' he said. 'Asked me the other day to get a dishwasher.' There was a pause, presumably to allow me to comprehend fully the ridiculousness of this idea.

'Right, so,' he continued. 'Aunt Jessica. From what I understand, she was always delicate as a girl. Bit of a waste of space, dreamy, always poorly for one reason or another. Read a lot, dabbled in watercolours – some of them are upstairs, bloody awful. Wasn't one for parties or young chaps. Her mind was always elsewhere – on higher things.' He made a derisive noise through the nostrils. 'Her brother married and left home, and she ended up caring for her parents. In those days they lived up north somewhere. Cheshire, was it?'

How the hell did I know? I made a small shrug – it seemed appropriate – and nodded at him to continue. Or maybe you could die, I thought, you grubby old pervert. Pop off right now, in some quiet and not-too-messy manner, and I could put the telly on.

'Anyway, the parents both kick the bucket – I think one of them topped themselves or something – and she inherits quite a nice amount, along with a decent bit of property. Ends up meeting some fellow in the City, falls in love and marries him. He was very different, by all accounts. First one round here to own a motor car, bit of a drinker. Eye for the ladies. They sold the family property and bought this place – he could get the train to London and she liked the rural bliss. Whether she liked it or not, she was effectively lady of the manor. In those days people still knew their place, and this was by far the biggest property around. I suppose we're talking the 1920s, something like that.

'In Aunt Jessica's day the house had much bigger grounds – we sold some land off – and most of the houses around here hadn't been built. The main road was more of a country lane. Bloody difficult to get a car down – I don't know how he managed to get to the station.

'All went well for a while, until she miscarried – or perhaps the baby died. I don't know: bit of a taboo subject in the family. But the relationship never recovered. And for whatever reason, having children was no longer a possibility.

'You get the picture. He's hardly here, she's a bit lost, time on her hands. She's trying to get herself together after whatever happened, but her husband isn't any support. Clearly, the marriage hasn't got much going for it.'

He paused and raised a tangled eyebrow, to check he still had an audience. I did my best to look attentive.

'So, this is what happened. I got the whole thing from Aunt Jessica's housekeeper, Martha, who lived in the house and became her closest companion towards the end. She still lived in the village when I was young, and I talked to her quite a bit. Those years with my aunt were so vivid in her mind.

'Here's the story – I hope I tell it a little more elegantly than poor old Martha.

'You can imagine the scene. It's a summer afternoon, quiet, and Jessica's husband, Edmund, is out at work. There's a knock on the door and Martha answers it. Then after a while she calls Jessica.

'The chap at the door is what you might call a gentleman of the road. Martha's done her best to get rid of him, but he insists on speaking to the lady of the house. Extraordinary-looking fellow. Stinks to high heaven of course. Filthy, as you'd expect, but quite well-spoken. Tall, but stooped, with a wide-brimmed hat with a pheasant feather in the band. He has a greasy old coat made of red velvet – a few brass buttons left on it – and some kind of voluminous canvas bag with all his worldly goods inside it. Boots falling apart, a wild-looking beard and intense, knowing eyes. It was the eyes Martha remembered most – and the monkey.'

'Monkey?' I said. It hadn't taken old Francis long to get into full storytelling mode. I knew he'd had a couple of novels published in his more vigorous years, although they were long out of print. He'd obviously told this yarn a few times before – maybe even worked it into one of his books. I thought I'd interrupt the flow, make him work a bit on the detail.

'Yes, a monkey,' he said, not missing a beat. 'Obviously it was a way of attracting a crowd and earning money. Martha said it ran all over the old man, sometimes hiding in his coat, sometimes perched on his shoulder. He kept a hoard of titbits for it, somewhere in his pockets. It was on a long, fine chain, attached to a red collar. And it had a gold earring – just like the old man. They must have been quite a sight in those days.

'Anyway, where were we? Oh yes. Jessica comes to the door and the man takes off his hat. The monkey immediately leaps on to his head and starts grooming itself. "Good afternoon, ma'am," says the old man.

'"Good afternoon," says Jessica, warily. Martha has stationed herself down the hall, pretending to rearrange some flowers, able to witness everything.

'"Now," says the old fellow. "I get around a fair bit. But you'll excuse me" – he gives a little bow – "I think I'm safe in saying we've not come across one another before."

'He pauses, and she gives a small nod in agreement. Like they were meeting at a dinner party, according to Martha. "They call me Sanders," the tramp says.

'"I'm Mrs Gresham," Jessica says. "And what can I do for you?"

'The old chap strokes his chin for a while, as if he's taking the name in. "Well," he says, and pauses again. He takes off his hat and raises his head. His eyes – they were surprisingly bright and clear – look directly into Jessica's and hold them for a moment. "You look to me like a lady with a proper measure of concern for her fellow creatures," he says, replacing his hat and settling it comfortably. "What would go down very nicely would be a glass of water."

'Jessica turns round to look for Martha. Jessica suddenly looks unsteady, unsure of herself. A bit adrift. Just for a second, she has to lean on the table there.' Uncle Francis gestured towards the hallway. 'Then she gathers herself and asks Martha to bring a folding garden chair, a jug of water and a glass for their visitor.

'These are brought – with some reluctance – and the old fellow gets himself settled on the chair, on the porch, and knocks back some water.

'Then Jessica remembers a bowl of cherries in the drawing room, and poor old Martha has to trot off and get those too – and not too happy about it.

'This Sanders character picks out a few cherries for the monkey and then takes some himself. The monkey tucks in, juice staining the fur around its mouth.

'"Well," says the tramp, once the cherries have gone. "We've been walking all day, looking for a bit of work, and not had much luck to speak of. Have we, little one?" he says, addressing the monkey, which has spat out the cherry stones and is now dozing in his lap. It opens its eyes, scratches itself and then settles down again.

'"So, I heard down in the village that the big house had a new lady owner, and I thought to myself that maybe me and the youngster here" – he indicates the monkey – "might pay a visit." He looks around, taking in his surroundings, as if he's thinking: Well, you can certainly spare a bob or two.

'"Well, we don't have any work here," says Jessica. "My gardener does all the odd jobs, I'm afraid."

'"Now that's a shame, but there's nothing to be done about it," says Sanders. "Still, we're very grateful for a chance to sit ourselves down for a while and have a bite to eat." He starts shifting about and preparing to haul himself up. Clearly, this is difficult. Once on his feet, he winces and pulls a dirty handkerchief out from somewhere to wipe his forehead.

'"No, no," says Jessica. "Please. Let me get you something a bit more filling. Just a moment –" and she's off into the hall, telling Martha to get a sandwich and a pot of tea together. Martha isn't happy, and hisses to Jessica that the tramp – and that horrible creature – could be helping themselves to anything in the house while they're out of sight. But she agrees to prepare something.

'Jessica hovers about giving instructions while Martha assembles the refreshments. Then they go back to the porch to find the old man and monkey in the same position as before.

'"Actually, best if we're off," says Sanders, turning, and the monkey jumps on his shoulder.

'"No," says Jessica, "please. There's some tea and a sandwich in the kitchen. Please."

'The tramp seems to consider the offer, and then turns into the house. He limps quite badly as he walks down the hall, peering at the paintings and the ornaments, stopping to touch a flower in Martha's fresh arrangement.

'He tucks into the sandwiches and the tea, and a few other things that Jessica persuades Martha to get out, and when he makes his way to the door afterwards, she once more notices the limp. She insists on giving him the name of her doctor in the nearby town, and tells him to get it looked at. She'll deal with any expenses.

'At this offer, Sanders just nods, pursing his cracked old lips, taking it in. Then, on the threshold, he says: "Again, we're very grateful to you ma'am. Sometimes it's not an easy life, being on the road, and we're thankful. And we'd like you to have this."

'He pulls out a carving he's made of a hare – that one there.' The thumb jerked over the shoulder again. 'And he gives it to her, with no more words, and shambles off down the drive, monkey on his shoulder.'

I hoped that was the end of the story. But no, Uncle Francis was simply pausing – for emphasis maybe, or simply to refill his glass. I made a show of picking up mine and draining the few drops left in the bottom. Telling his story had got him quite animated. But he still ignored the hint.

'Jessica and the housekeeper don't see eye to eye about the episode, but eventually things smooth over and life gets back to normal. Until the next visit.

'This time it's a much younger man, with a straw hat, a roll to sleep on and a bag of tools. Again, he says he's looking for work, and again Martha does her best to get rid of him. Like old Sanders, he insists on seeing the lady of the house. According to Martha, it's like he's expecting something. Again, a meal is provided, along with a blanket from the summer house. Before leaving, he gives Jessica a clothes peg made into a doll.

'That's in there somewhere too,' said Uncle Francis, once more indicating the cabinet, 'along with all the others.'

I got up and took a closer look at them. There were around thirty in all. Maybe the story had a grain of truth in it, but on the other hand, any old fool could assemble such a collection from flea markets and antiques fairs. 'So all these things were given to Jessica by tramps?' I asked.

'Oh yes,' said Uncle Francis. 'Tramps, beggars, misfits of all kinds. It went on for a year or so. Every few weeks usually. Old drunks, young Gypsy types, peddlers, salesmen down on their luck, your full range of waifs and strays and low-lifes. A couple of women too. One towing a child behind her, with a yarn about being a widow and being turfed out for not being able to pay the rent. That one was told to buy some clothes for the kid in town, and have the bill sent to Jessica. None of these people were local, mind you. All travelling through, on foot, in all weathers.

'Most people would have sent them packing, of course, but Jessica had a welcome and some small act of kindness for the lot of them. All of them gave her some kind of gift in return, and she began putting them in that cabinet. And do you know what the really odd thing was?'

I shook my head. Do tell, I thought. Get on with it. Any chance of watching some telly tonight was disappearing fast.

'They didn't know each other, these people. Every time, she asked them: Had they met an old man with a monkey? Or had someone told them about this house? And they all said no – they just called in as they passed through.

'And when she asked Martha and the gardener, who had worked at the house before Jessica's time, they told her they had never known the place to attract such visitors.

'Aunt Jessica pondered these things in her heart, as they say. I'm afraid, being one of nature's sensitive souls, she pondered them a bit too much.

'She already spent a lot of time on her own, with her husband, Edmund, working all day and with his own leisure pursuits to follow. But now she became even more self-absorbed. According to Martha she wasn't exactly unhappy, more preoccupied, like she was guarding something wonderful and fragile inside her – some private truth that needed constant nurture. She would drift around the garden or read for hours, jolted back into reality when Martha approached her, as gently as she could, to bring her a cup of tea or remind her to take a meal. Or when the doorbell rang.

'She took to going to church in the village, which she'd never done before. Martha was a churchgoer and Jessica asked if she could go with her. She'd sit through the whole service with a beatific expression on her face. The ladies in the congregation were excited to have her join them at first, but soon gave up trying to engage her in conversation.

'One Sunday, when she and Martha were leaving after communion, she stopped at the church door to congratulate the vicar on his sermon. Then she leant in close. "I've got my flock too, you know," Martha heard her say. "They're scattered far and wide. But they're guided to me."

'The vicar was so concerned that he called round to the house and had a word with her husband. But Edmund couldn't get much sense out of her. Eventually, Martha told me, he just warned her to be careful and told her she couldn't just invite anyone into the house. But his interests were elsewhere, and he began to stay up in London a couple of times a week.

'Things nearly came to head one Saturday morning before Christmas, however, when he noticed a cashmere scarf of his had gone missing. Not only that, but his whisky supply had been noticeably depleted.

'Martha recalled the episode very clearly, because it was the first time the couple had rowed so badly.

'Here's how it happened. Jessica has finally emerged from her room and is picking at a very late breakfast.

Edmund stomps in and sits down opposite her. When Martha approaches with fresh coffee he waves it away. "Where's my blue scarf?" he demands.

Jessica considers this for a moment. "I think I gave it to a man who came to the house," she says eventually. "He was cold." She looks up at Edmund with a hopeful smile, as if she's expecting to see understanding – as if she's given explanation enough. "It's freezing outside," she adds. But he suddenly shoves his chair back and stands up, making her start as his hands slam on to the table. Martha retreats to the hall.

'"A cashmere scarf!" Martha hears Edmund say. "And I suppose you sat him down and gave him a nice tot of my bloody Scotch as well, did you?"

'"Well, yes," says Jessica. "Martha said not to, but do you know, it was just what he needed. He'd walked for miles, he told me. He was so grateful. He said –"

'"I don't give a toss what he said. What the hell are you doing, handing out my clothes and my single malt to complete bloody strangers? Scroungers and criminals?"

'"They're not," says Jessica. "They come to me. They're sent to me. I –" But he turns and strides into the hall, snatching up his motoring gloves and another scarf. Martha hears the door slam shut, and goes to see how Jessica is. She's still sitting at the breakfast table, her fingers pressed gently to her temples. She pushes her plate away, takes one sip of coffee, and gets up from the table. Edmund is gone for the rest of the day.

'After that, Martha began to worry a great deal. Jessica was becoming ever more solitary, more disconnected. She would spend long periods on a sofa: eyes closed, lips silently moving, her lids fluttering open when asked if she wanted a cup of tea or some food. She would take a drink, occasionally fruit, but rarely ate a substantial meal. She became thin, fragile, but with a bright nervous energy that leapt into life when one of her wanderers arrived.

'Martha was also concerned about the number of items going missing. She kept a careful eye on Jessica's callers, and gave them a stern look on the doorstep that left them in no doubt that she was alert to any funny business. She recruited the gardener to her cause, but neither could be on guard all the time. She was forced to spend time in the kitchen, making tea or snacks for Jessica's latest acquaintance, while the gardener didn't work every day, and had enough to do when he was there.

'Martha soon realised that the visitors were being given access to the house – allowed to use one of the bathrooms, for example – when her back was turned. And whatever opportunities they were being given, it was clear they were taking advantage of them. Items of silver cutlery disappeared. A candlestick went missing. An ornament here or there. An expensive pen left on the bureau in the hall. Once, a bottle of brandy.

'To protect Jessica, Martha tried to keep Edmund ignorant of these losses, often simply replacing missing items using the household budget controlled by his wife.

'It was easy for her to get authority from Jessica for such spending. She was becoming increasingly ethereal, less and less involved with the daily routine. Edmund, too, was hardly engaged with the running of the house. His overnight stays at his London club became more frequent. At weekends he would play golf or motor off to the south coast. He noticed the missing pen, but Martha told him it was simply lost somewhere in the house, and by the time he looked for it again she had managed to order a new one.

'He spent less and less time with his wife. Occasionally, she would accompany him to social events, but these came up rarely.

'It was clear to Martha that she was observing the collapse of a marriage and a rapid decline in her mistress.

'When she told me this part of the story, she got herself ridiculously distressed, as if it had all happened yesterday. I had to wait for her to pull herself together. Then it all came out in a flood. I won't do the awful Oxfordshire accent, but it was quite a speech.

'"Jessica had so much love to give, so much tenderness," Martha told me, "but she didn't know the world. She didn't know how people were. Mr Edmund was never there, and when he was they hardly talked. He showed that motor car of his more affection than he did her. And what else had she got in life? If she'd have had children, she'd have had a proper purpose – somewhere for all that love to go."

'What really concerned Martha were Jessica's visitors. "So many… *people* were coming to the house," she told me. "Wanderers, Jessica called them. Lost souls. I know what I called them. She was playing the Good Samaritan to them and they were taking advantage, they were. Scoffing meals, washing off their filth in the downstairs bathroom, all newly fitted out and beautiful, and more often than not helping themselves to a little souvenir or a slug of his nibs's Scotch. And who had to make the meals, and clean up after them, and make sure she wasn't interfered with, or bashed over the head? Muggins here, that's who."

'Martha had good reason to be worried. By the summer, Jessica had stopped leaving the house altogether – not even to go to church. Even Edmund began to be concerned. He called in some fashionable nerve doctor, who spent an hour and a half examining her. All he could do was prescribe some pills and advise fresh air, regular meals and mild social diversions.

The vicar came to see her too. He was no fool: he had years of experience of the everyday dramas of a rural congregation. But that couldn't help him here. Like Martha and Edmund, he couldn't penetrate Jessica's inner world, or challenge her glowing certainties. All he could do was warn her to take care.

'Martha saw him to the door. "I'm not sure what I can do," he said. "I told her the Lord expects us to be hospitable. But we must look after ourselves too."'

Uncle Francis paused again. The old bastard could certainly tell a tale, I had to give him that. 'So what happened?' I asked.

'Jessica faded away. She had one or two more visitors, but became weaker and weaker, ate less and less, and was taken off to a sanatorium in Eastbourne, I think it was. She died there soon afterwards. Edmund did visit her a couple of times. She's buried here, you know, in the churchyard. Quite a tasteful memorial.'

Uncle Francis lapsed briefly into silence before announcing 'More wine,' and plodding unsteadily down the hall.

The doorbell rang. I ignored it, assuming the old sod would get it. He didn't, so I called out that there was someone at the door. There was no response – he was obviously occupied in the recesses of the house. So when the bell rang again I went to answer it.

A dowdy middle-aged woman stood there, holding something covered in a tea towel.

'Oh,' she said, flustered. 'Is Francis in?'

'Yes, but he's busy I'm afraid.'

'Oh. Only, I just popped round with this.' She lifted the cloth, revealing a half-decent-looking apple crumble. 'Sorry, I'm Evelyn, from the next house down. I thought I'd do him a pudding.'

'So, shall I take it?'

'Well, yes, I suppose so. Thanks. It's just a crumble, but I know he likes them. Tell him there's no rush to get the dish back.'

'OK, bye.'

'Bye now, nice to meet you. Make sure you get a taste!'

I closed the door and put the dish in the kitchen. I met Francis in the hall.

'Who was that?' he asked. 'Collecting for bloody something, were they? Every sodding week I get one ringing the bell. They don't get a penny out of me. If I spot them coming down the drive I don't even answer.'

'No, it was a lady from down the road. Evelyn, I think. Gave you an apple crumble – I put it in the kitchen.'

He pondered this. 'Well, no idea what prompted that,' he said. 'I try not to have anything to do with the woman. But it'll do for pudding tomorrow, I suppose. Don't mind a bit of crumble.'

He stumped off into the living room with the Malbec. No crumble for the long-lost relative then.

He filled his glass and promptly emptied it in a couple of draughts. He smacked his lips and filled it to the brim again. Then it seemed to dawn on him that I might want some. 'More?' he asked. I nodded, and received half a glass.

'Aah... Now,' he said, settling back into his chair, 'I was going to bring you up to date. Aunt Jessica and so on.'

There was no pause for my assent.

'So, when I took this place on it was in a bit of a state. Did a lot of the work on it myself, clearing the garden and getting ivy off everything. I was out by the front gate, stripping the ivy off the wall there, when I found something.'

He looked up to check I was still listening.

'It was a small mark, scratched on to a brick. Very worn, so I couldn't make it out, but something like a circle with crossed lines in the middle.' He paused and shot me a glance. 'I don't know if you know, but I had a bit of trouble with the college...'

I shook my head. 'Hmmph,' he continued. 'Anyway, there was one of those situations that get completely misinterpreted these days, and then there's no telling anyone what really happened. You haven't got a bloody chance. I was giving a tutorial in Old English in my room, the last week of term, helping one of my students out.

'I offered her a bit of the college sherry – end of term and all that. Had a couple myself, of course. I was reading out a section of Beowulf – you know, the big battle with Grendel's mother – and waving my arms about a bit too much, trying to convey the drama. Apparently, so the official version went, I stumbled. Into her lap. All I remember doing was putting a hand out to steady myself, but it was my word against hers, and the man's story is never given any credence these days. So that was that. Anyway, where was I?'

'A mark on the wall.'

He took another large glass of Malbec. 'Oh yes. So, for the time being, while all this was going on with the college, I still had access to the library. I had a fair bit of time on my hands, and I thought I'd do some research on that old mark. It seems that until quite recently, tramps would leave marks on buildings, as a guide to others who came that way. They'd leave a sign warning there was a dangerous dog, or that a copper lived in the house. Or, they'd indicate that it was worthwhile calling there.'

'And the mark you found?'

'Well, it's not entirely clear. It could mean: "Worth calling: owner is kind and generous." Or it could mean: "Worth trying your luck: lots of stuff to steal." Or both.'

There was a silence. 'Well, I'm off to bed,' he said after a while. 'You'll be OK seeing yourself off in the morning?'

'Oh yes.'

'Good. And, ah, good luck. With the interview.'

'Yes, thanks. And thanks for putting me up.'

'Hmmph.'

He took a step, as if to leave the room, then stopped and looked back. He nodded in the direction of the Malbec on the small table by his armchair. There was maybe a glassful left.

'Help yourself,' he said. 'Finish it off if you like.'

Vanishing point

Muldoon put his substantial shoulder to the door. Thompson flinched as wood split and splintered. He flinched again, as the warm fug of the room rushed into the corridor and hit them. Neither man acknowledged the almost sickening surge of relief that washed over them along with the acrid, imprisoned air. It was clear from a quick scan, just standing at the threshold of the tiny room, that whatever secrets the locked door had been concealing, a corpse was not one of them.

They stepped through the mangled doorway. Thompson picked a sliver of cheap timber from the sleeve of his suit jacket and brushed the smooth fabric with his hand, twice.

'OK, you were right,' he said. 'Locked from the inside. No wonder the master key didn't work.' He paused and examined the damage to the door frame. 'You going to sort this out from your budget?'

Muldoon wore a polo shirt with the university logo and cargo pants. He rubbed a tattooed bicep then turned his big head to Thompson. 'It's a Student Welfare thing, isn't it?' he said. 'You're Student Welfare. All I did was get you in, like you wanted. I'll get my lads to fix it, but it's not coming out of Maintenance, mate.'

'OK,' said Thompson. He was not going to argue with a guy who could do that with one heave of his shoulder. 'Finance can work it out. The main thing is, what the hell's he been up to? You think he locked the door and climbed out the window for a laugh?'

They went further in. A single bed, unmade and covered in books, occupied almost the full length of the wall to their right. At its foot, near the door, was a small wash basin. Opposite the bed were a desk, chair and chest of drawers. Coke cans, a grubby mug and a plate encrusted with food occupied one half of the desk, a laptop the other. A pair of jeans, a hoodie and a variety of T-shirts were draped over the chair. Underwear lay in a pile beneath it. Facing the door was a window.

Standard first-year room, fairly standard level of detritus and attention to hygiene. Nothing unusual, except for the fact that no one had seen its occupant, one Michael Andrewes, first-year chemistry student, for three days. And what was on the wall. Which explained the chemical tang to the air. Freshly dried paint.

OK, I suppose I let it get out of hand. I know I'm doing chemistry, like my mum and dad wanted me to, but I always thought, maybe I could have done art instead. The kids at school – I didn't have a great time there – they were like, 'You're not Michael Andrewes, you're Michelangelo', ha ha, big LOLs, just because I was good at art. It was the only reason I went to school. I had a few issues, you could say. Some days my parents had to prise me out of my bedroom and force me out of the door. I didn't have any friends. I had no one to talk to, but I could pick up a brush and start painting and my feelings, all the stuff inside, would come out, on the paper, in the paint and in the colours. And the other kids used to take the piss, but I got an A. And then it was uni, and chemistry, and I sort of forgot about art, especially when me and Gemma got together.

It was so nice, being with someone else, and she bought me a poster of Van Gogh's Sunflowers *and we put it up over the bed and we'd look at it when we were cuddled up in there, and say when we finished uni we were going to go round Europe. Maybe France and see the sunflower fields, she said, and I said yes, or maybe Norway and Iceland and those places and see the fjords with the big waterfalls and maybe even the Northern Lights. But then we had, like, a massive row, and she split up with me, and she pulled the picture off the wall, really pulled it, ripped it a bit, and some of the plaster came away with the drawing pin, and left a hole. So I thought I'd better get some filler to fix the hole, and some paint and a brush to hide the damage. But after I put a coat of paint on, you could still see where the hole was, so I put a bit more paint on, and then – I can't remember if I really thought it through – I got some more paint and I thought, you know, why not paint* something*? Do a painting. Get my emotions out and make myself feel better and stop thinking about Gemma. And then...*

'Whooh,' said Muldoon. 'He's been busy. That'll take some covering up.'

The large abstract painting was a swirl of colour and cascading light, with a still, dark void at its heart. In the blackness was a tiny human figure, almost lost in a galaxy of chaos.

'What do you think it is?' said Thompson.

'No idea. Storm at sea?'

'Yeah, could be,' said Thompson, running a finger across the still tacky surface. 'Or, tell you what it reminds me of. One of those photos they take with that big space telescope.'

'Or what do they have up by the Arctic,' said Muldoon, 'those lights you can only see if you're way up north? Aurora something. Could be those?'

Turning, he realised his companion's attention was now fixed on the window.

'Look,' said Thompson, 'it's bloody locked. How the hell did he get out?'

Yes, I know it got out of control. I kept painting, adding more and more, then painting over what I'd painted and starting again, making it bigger, making it something I really wanted to paint, something I had *to paint, and I ended up painting all night, nearly, as well as all day, and not going to classes. I knew I had to finish it, but it was really hard, because I'd think it was finished, then kind of doze off, and then wake up feeling so bad, and it would help to start again, to make it better, to make it… complete, make it hold everything going on in my head. It was the dream we'd had. And it was the nightmare I was going through. And then I saw that it needed just one more thing. It needed a person. So I got a small brush and reached out, into the colours whirling all around me, and there was a blank, empty stillness right in the middle.*

And I put myself in it.

CPSIA information can be obtained
at www.ICGtesting.com
Printed in the USA
LVHW021528090122
708114LV00021B/2115